Pride Publishing books by L.M. Somerton:

The Portrait
Black Dog
Stroke Rate
Mountain Rescue

Tales from The Edge Volume One
Reaching the Edge
Living on the Edge

Tales from The Edge Volume Two
Dancing on the Edge
A Double-Edged Sword

Tales from The Edge Volume Three
Rough Around the Edges
Scorched Edges

Investigating Love
Rasputin's Kiss
Evil's Embrace
Tarot's Touch

The Wyverns
Mantrap
Deathtrap

What's his Passion?
Picturing Lysander
Testing Lysander

Anthologies
Racing Hearts: Keeping the Luck In

STROKE RATE

L.M. SOMERTON

Stroke Rate
ISBN # 978-1-78651-867-5
©Copyright L.M. Somerton 2016
Cover Art by Posh Gosh ©Copyright February 2016
Interior text design by Claire Siemaszkiewicz
Pride Publishing

Published in 2016 by Pride Publishing, Newland House, The Point, Weaver Road, Lincoln, LN6 3QN, United Kingdom.

STROKE RATE

Dedication

To pushing limits.

Chapter One

The October sun had dipped below the horizon some time since, and the distinct nip of autumn pervaded the air. The river was a black silk ribbon twisting sinuously toward the distant lights of the town—not really that far away but it could have been another world. The silence of the riverbank was broken only by the whisper of long grass and the occasional splash of a coot diving for cover amid the reeds.

It was the commotion of a startled bird that broke the reverie of the young man standing in the darkness. He gently flipped the small, smooth pebble that he had been turning over and over in his hand into the water. The resulting ripples caught the light reflected from the window of the building behind him. A slight smile flickered across his soft lips as he mused on the consequences that one small action could invoke. He sighed and turned away from the water. It had been a while since anything—or anyone—had created ripples in the monotony of his life.

A few steps took him to a low door that was slightly ajar, with warm light spilling around the edges as if trying to illuminate the night. At six feet tall, he had to duck his head as he slipped inside and pulled the door closed behind him. The small door he had used was cut into a much larger set that took up the whole wall. He breathed in the familiar smell of the boathouse. The wooden Edwardian structure had a smell all its own — oils and varnish mixed with the more modern scents of neoprene and acrylic paint, overlaid by the light fragrance of cedar and oak.

Okeanos Rowing Club owned an impressive set of immaculate boats that were racked along the walls. One full side stored the 'sweep' boats, where each rower has one oar. There were three eight-seaters and a range of single, double and quad boats all cradled by sturdy metal frames that could be cranked up the walls to provide more storage capacity. On the other side were the 'sculling' boats, which were all single and double seat arrangements. At the far end of the shed there was a trailer, pre-loaded with racing kayaks. They always had to be transported to other venues, so they stayed on their trailer, ready to go. The general equipment store could be reached through another door, and there were also two changing rooms with basic shower facilities at the back of the building.

Benedict Astor contemplated the view. Everything was in place, as it should be. Of course it was — after all, he was the one who had heaved and shoved every sodding boat into position, just as he had done virtually every night for the last six months. He rolled his shoulders and rubbed his aching arms before wandering over to the notice board to read the roughly scrawled note pinned there.

Ben — Extra jobs for tonight — clean the drain in the men's locker room, sand the front step (it's splintering again) and refill the water coolers.

S.

"Just wonderful," Ben muttered quietly.

That was another hour's work at least, and it was already late. Ben used his long, slim fingers to tease at the knots in his collar-length hair before kneading away the tension in his tight neck muscles. He had an idea why Sebastian Cooke, the rowing club's president, had it in for him — but he wasn't sure, and it certainly wasn't something he was prepared to discuss with the man. It was easier just to put up with the never-ending list of menial tasks and hard labor that Seb took great delight in sending his way.

He tackled the worst job first, donning rubber gloves to remove the locker room drain cover and pull out the accumulated muck. He managed not to gag too much at the smell, then dumped half a bottle of bleach down the hole. The locker room now smelled like the inside of a hospital but even that was a distinct improvement. After replacing the plastic grating over the drain he peeled off the gloves and dumped them in the mop bucket. Next, he heaved three water bottles for the coolers out of the storage cupboard and replaced the half-empty ones, even though they didn't really need changing. Finally, he got down on his hands and knees and applied a piece of coarse sandpaper to the front step. Rowers, including him, often carried the boats back up from the river with bare feet, so this was one job he didn't mind doing. He'd gotten a splinter in his heel once and it had been not only uncomfortable, but also difficult to get out.

The sanding was strangely therapeutic, if hard on his fingers, and it gave him time to wonder—for the thousandth time—if the job was really worth it. He came to the same conclusion he always did. It was temporary. It wouldn't be forever, and three hours of labor a day wasn't a big price to pay for free accommodation and club membership. The tiny flat above the boat room wasn't much, but it was quiet and private, plus he could cycle along the riverside path to get to the university each day. Even at student rates there was no way he would have been able to afford the fees at Okeanos otherwise and he needed to row. The river kept him grounded and at peace.

A lapse in concentration cost him three grazed knuckles as the sandpaper slipped across his hand instead of the wood beneath it. He swore softly and sucked specks of blood off his skin before shaking away the pain.

"Enough."

The rough edge of the step was sanded smooth. Tiredly, he packed up everything he had been using, brushed an errant strand of hair from his eyes, then locked up. It was after ten and he had to be out of bed to open up at five-thirty. Even at this time of year, the early rowers would be arriving by six and Seb would have his hide if everything wasn't ready for them. The upside of the unsociable hours was that he could take a single scull out and have the river to himself for a while before anyone else got onto the water.

The boathouse flat was really little more than a bedsit, but Ben had made it as cozy as he could. His bed was covered with a warm patchwork quilt that was a little twee, but he felt that style could be sacrificed for comfort and warmth. Bright throws in autumnal colors covered the battered sofa and single armchair positioned in front of the wood burner. There was a small galley kitchen, and a desk and bookcase tucked into a corner. A tiny bathroom that didn't actually house a bath, just a temperamental shower, took up the only remaining space. He could always use the club facilities when it played up, though, so it didn't bother him too much.

Ben made a hot, milky cup of cocoa and spent a couple of hours working on an essay that was due in a few days. He was reading literature, and though the course didn't require many contact hours with his lecturers, the schedule of reading and written work was demanding. His tutor also had a reputation as an utter bastard who never gave extensions and was overly fond of his red pen — handing the essay in late just wouldn't be worth the aggravation. Ben didn't enjoy confrontation of any kind. His inherent need to please made him an effective peacekeeper and he had no wish to develop the kind of wild boy reputation that some of his peers seemed to delight in.

When his eyelids started drooping and his pen clattered to the desk from his slack fingers, he knew it was time to get to bed. He stripped off his clothes and stretched slowly, gradually releasing the tension from his muscles. Half asleep, he padded to the bathroom and went through his evening routine, grimacing at his reflection. His hair, as always, needed a trim and he looked as tired as he felt. The blue-gray shadows beneath his eyes attested to his fatigue. He preferred to sleep naked unless it was absolutely freezing, and climbed beneath the covers with a sigh. It would be nice to have a warm body to snuggle up against but Ben was very reserved and not interested in casual relationships. He was too shy to approach anyone he didn't know and the entire concept of dating was both mysterious and terrifying. His ideal man had to be out there somewhere, but for now he was limited to what his own imagination could provide.

Chapter Two

"Season of mists and mellow fruitfulness, my arse."

Ben shivered and muttered to himself as he unlocked the boathouse door the next morning and peered through fog that would not have been out of place in *The Hound of the Baskervilles*. The sun was not yet up, and he could feel the heavy dew soaking through his canvas shoes as he pulled open the large doors that granted access to the boats. He removed all the padlocks that secured the racks, then lifted down the oldest single scull—the one he always used. He made light work of carrying it to the water, since his muscles were used to the demands of moving the boats around. At the river's edge, he slipped off his shoes, climbed into the boat carefully and made himself as comfortable as possible on the hard seat. He was wearing plain, navy blue Lycra shorts—because they didn't get in the way of the oars—and an ancient rugby shirt. He hated the vanity of some crews with their expensive, matching kits. He just wanted to row. Plain and simple. That didn't require a fancy wardrobe, just muscle power and endurance.

He pushed the boat gently away from the bank and settled into a relaxed position, ensuring he was well balanced. It wasn't unusual for scullers to end up in the water after becoming unseated. The first pull of the oars always made him smile as the river fought the power of his muscles, but soon the boat was slicing through the water and he lost himself to the rhythm of long, clean strokes. Anyone watching might have thought it was effortless, but Ben was testing every muscle in his body. The natural resistance of the current was challenging. He rowed hard for fifteen minutes before turning the boat and retracing his journey, slowing only to cool down over the last few hundred meters. He steadied himself with some deep breaths before expertly maneuvering his scull into the shallows, then disembarking. The bank was now crawling with rowers and someone else eager to get out on the water commandeered the boat. Ben kept the craft steady while its new occupant got settled, then strolled back to the boathouse, carrying his shoes and responding to greetings with a nod or a shy smile here and there.

Several of the girls gave him a second or even third glance, though they all knew damn well he wouldn't be interested. It didn't seem to matter—he'd been told he was pretty to look at and Lycra left little to the imagination. Self-consciously, Ben tugged at the hem of his top and resolved to find something longer to wear over his shorts.

He ducked his head and avoided eye contact as much as possible as he wove between boats and crews preparing on the path. He made it to the boathouse without tripping over anything, which in his view was a success. He looked up and had to suppress a groan. Seb was standing there waiting—hands on hips, a sulky look on his face. He would have been reasonably good-looking if he ever managed to smile, but Ben had yet to witness that momentous event.

Ben shifted from foot to foot and wished that he had something to hold in front of him. Seb's eyes continually drifted downwards, as if by magnetic attraction, and Ben had to wonder if the man's girlfriend had ever noticed what he was looking at. Probably not—she was too self-obsessed to worry about Seb's secret inclinations. Anyway, he was so firmly in the closet that the door was locked, bolted and probably needed some kind of iris scan to get into. Ben shuddered at the thought of ever being touched by those big, hairy-backed hands. *Ugh!* He tried to focus on thinking of something polite to say but, as usual, his tongue was not as proficient as his mind and he could only manage a mumbled, "Good morning."

"Where the fuck have you been?" Seb snapped.

Ben resisted the urge to roll his eyes and make a sarcastic retort. He knew damn well that Seb couldn't care less where he had been—he was just pissed off that Ben hadn't been around to abuse when he'd arrived.

"I was on the riv—"

"Whatever. I've got to be out in the eight in five minutes. I just wanted to tell you that I've put you down for a promise."

Shit. Ben was tempted to pretend that he had misheard, but it couldn't have been clearer. The club was holding a promise auction to raise some funds, and he had been resisting the pressure to offer a promise for weeks now. It wasn't that he didn't want to support the fundraising effort—it was just that the club's members were, in the main, filthy rich and were promising all kinds of great things. Weekends in the parents' holiday home, products from family companies and farms… Ben just didn't have anything to offer that wouldn't look pathetic in comparison. What the hell had Seb done?

"Don't look so fucking worried – it's not going to cost you anything. Well, not in cash anyway." Seb smirked unpleasantly. "You've promised twenty-four hours of your labor. One day where you do whatever the winning bidder wants you to do." Seb raised a sandy eyebrow expectantly.

"It's not a slave auction, Seb. That's not the idea."

In his mind, Ben was calling the club's president all the rude names he could think of. *Bastard. He probably has plans to bid for me himself.* There was no way out, though – to refuse would look really bad, and he didn't have anything else to offer. He'd just have to hope that one of the girls' mothers would want some gardening done or the bloody Merc washed. He didn't mind the work – what turned Ben's stomach was the thought of what Seb might have him do if his was the winning bid.

He looked up into a pair of cruel, mud-colored eyes. Seb opened his mouth, then just as quickly clamped it closed again. His attention was no longer fixed on Ben, but on something or someone behind him. Ben knew that there was only one person, other than Seb's domineering mother, who could shut him up that fast.

"Astor, I need a second for the double scull. Get down to the water." The voice was as cold and hard as polished granite.

Ben's stomach twisted itself into more knots. This day was getting progressively crappier and it wasn't even seven a.m.

"Lucien, I'm sure we can find you someone more qualified…" Seb's tone was obsequious enough to make Ben feel like vomiting.

"If I wanted your opinion, Seb, I'd ask for it."

Ben turned and met a pair of deceptively soft blue eyes, the color of faded denim. Lucien Thorne was rowing aristocracy, with Olympic and world gold medals to his name. He was also real-life aristocracy, having become Lord Thorne of Keering after the death of his father the previous year. He was also Ben's secret fantasy material. He was an imposing figure, standing at six feet three, with the haughty bearing that only came with absolute self-confidence. He had the looks to go with his personality — sinister and brooding. Unruly black hair, so dark it had the blue sheen of a raven's wing, curled around his ears. His chin was dusted with dark stubble and his eyes were framed by thick lashes below eyebrows as inky as his hair. One of those eyebrows rose slightly as he pinned Ben with an icy glare.

"Why the fuck are you still standing here? Get your arse in the boat."

"I've been out already, Lucien," Ben said. He didn't want to let Lucien down because he couldn't keep pace.

"I know. Please don't make me repeat myself."

Ben flushed, which caused a slight twist to the corner of Lucien's lip, but did as he had been told and jogged down to the river. Two other rowers were holding the boat in place, so he climbed into the front seat and got comfortable. His arms were already aching from his earlier session and he knew that matching strokes with Lucien was not going to be easy. He closed his eyes, tried to relax his muscles and get into the right frame of mind for another demanding session on the water.

He had no idea why he had been chosen. He couldn't recall more than a couple of occasions over the last few months when Lucien had even spoken to him. He was normally very aloof and rowed only with the very best the club had to offer. Ben had no illusions about his own talent. He rowed for fun and knew that he was fortunate to have the build and strength to make him passably good. He was nowhere close to Lucien's standard, though.

"Wake up. You can't row if you're fucking sleeping."

A sharp tap to the side of his head snapped Ben's eyes open, but he had no time to protest the unwarranted accusation.

The boat hardly shifted as Lucien climbed onto the bow seat and crossed his arms, ready to pull back on the oars. Ben resisted the urge to snarl at him and mimicked his position as the boat was pushed gently out into the current. He was acutely aware of Lucien's taller frame close behind him, a dark shadow in the corner of his eye. He was wearing all black, and Ben couldn't remember ever seeing him in anything else. His legs were lightly tanned and it was easy to imagine him stretched out on the deck of a sleek yacht in the Mediterranean, which was probably where he had spent the summer.

"Ready?"

Ben was pretty sure that whether he was or not was irrelevant but he nodded anyway.

"Pull."

Lucien set a punishing pace, but Ben soon found that their bodies synchronized effortlessly, as if they had been rowing together for years. They had a similar, simple style, cutting the water cleanly and applying one hundred percent effort to the pull-through. It was physically demanding and Ben could feel the burn throughout his body as Lucien increased the stroke rate. He would have complained, but he needed every breath just to keep going. Stubborn pride would not allow him to give up.

By the time they got back to the clubhouse wharf, Ben thought he was going to die. It would have been a mercy. He leaned forward over the oars, every aching muscle contributing to an overriding sense of misery. Lucien must think him absolutely pathetic and, for some reason he couldn't quite fathom, that hurt almost as much as his tortured body. The narrow boat rocked slightly as Lucien got up behind him and stepped onto the bank. Ben looked up, fearing the worst—either a scathing glare or an angry figure striding away—but, to his amazement, Lucien offered a hand to help him out of the boat. Adrenaline still surged through his system and it seemed to enhance his vision as he took in slim fingers and a tanned arm darkened by a covering of soft hair. He didn't move straight away, and Lucien scowled impatiently.

"Get out of the fucking boat, Benedict. I'm not standing here all day."

Benedict? Christ, that was what his mother called him when he'd done something wrong. Most people assumed that his full name was Benjamin and it flashed through his mind that Lucien must have asked someone. *Why would he bother?*

Ben stood up shakily, thighs and calves burning from the build-up of lactic acid, and grabbed the proffered arm. He felt the muscles tense to balance his weight and the sensation sent a line of fire straight to his groin. He started to harden and immediately flushed, because there was no way his shorts were going to offer any concealment whatsoever. He tried to disengage himself but Lucien held his wrist firmly. His mild blue gaze drifted downwards, then lifted to meet Ben's eyes. Lucien's expression seemed to be more triumphant than angry and Ben waited for the inevitable cut-down.

Instead, he was towed up the grassy slope, then released.

"Six-thirty tomorrow morning. Don't be fucking late and don't go out on your own first. You'll need all your energy—I'm not going to go easy on you again."

Ben knew Lucien had been talking about rowing but it didn't seem that way. The undercurrent of his words seemed to suggest something entirely different, and Ben's body responded with an enthusiasm that gave him chills. Of course, it could just be the sweat drying on his body, but his rock-hard cock ached and Ben had to remove his gaze from Lucien's trim, black-clad arse before someone noticed that his tongue was hanging out. Metaphorically speaking.

He didn't understand his own attraction. Sure, Lucien was gorgeous and had a body to match, but he was an arrogant bastard who seemed to expect the entire world to bow down and do his bidding. He had all the charm of a great white shark with an empty stomach. Belatedly, Ben thought about protesting. Though painful, rowing with Lucien had been a joy, but the assumption that he would be available and willing to drop everything to show up again the next day was deeply irritating. Ben could probably catch up with him and refuse, but he sighed and allowed himself to accept that it would never happen. Something inside him had responded to that commanding tone and though he was ninety percent annoyed, the ten percent that mattered just wanted to comply.

Ben trudged back to the boathouse, ignoring the envious stares of other rowers. They wouldn't have been jealous if their muscles had been aching as much as his were. He knew that later he'd be so stiff and sore that cycling into college was going to be an endurance test rather than a pleasure. Lucien hadn't even looked out of breath, let alone in pain. It just wasn't fair.

Instead of using the club showers, Ben slipped upstairs to his own eccentric bathroom and stood beneath the sporadic shower spray with his eyes closed. He went through the motions of washing and shampooing on automatic pilot because all he could think of were Lucien's pretty eyes glaring at him. He grabbed a towel, wrapped it around his hips and strolled toward his tiny kitchen to get a bottle of water from the fridge.

"The towel suits you."

"What the hell…?"

Ben whirled around to see Lucien standing just inside his bedsit door, leaning nonchalantly against the wall. The sudden movement caused Ben's towel to slip, and he was left clutching nothing but a bottle of water to maintain his modesty.

He froze, aware of every cool drop of water that dripped from his hair and slid down his back and shoulders. A flush heated his cheeks, and all moisture seemed to have disappeared from his mouth.

Lucien gave a short, wicked laugh and Ben blushed to the roots of his hair. He would have to put down the bottle before he could pick up his towel, and against all reason his cock didn't seem to share his embarrassment and was swelling stubbornly. Lucien's gaze was unashamedly fixed on his body and Ben half expected him to come closer and touch. He picked the lesser of two evils, turned around and bent over to pick up the towel. He could hear Lucien clicking his tongue in annoyance, but Ben would be damned if he would give him any more encouragement. The clicking stopped, and the man seemed to be taking deep, slow breaths. When Ben turned back to face him, he half wondered if he was going to be pushed over the kitchen counter and fucked to within an inch of his life. He attempted to defuse the atmosphere with a tentative question.

"How did you get in here? This isn't part of the club."

Ben clutched the towel tightly against his body, as if terrified that it would endeavor to fall away again of its own accord.

"The door was open. Perhaps you were a little distracted when you came in and forgot to close it properly?"

Lucien walked slowly across the room until he was within touching distance of Ben's dripping body.

"I want you earlier tomorrow than I said. I came to let you know. Be ready at six."

It wasn't a request, and Lucien clearly did not expect any response. He reached out and caught a rolling droplet of water as it slid down Ben's smooth chest. He trailed his finger downwards to the edge of the towel, making only light contact but eliciting a tremble all the same. He met Ben's startled eyes, smirked, then turned and disappeared out of the door.

Ben let out a shuddering breath he hadn't realized he'd been holding. On legs that didn't seem to work properly anymore, he propelled himself toward his bed, where he flung himself down and started working his iron-hard cock desperately. He came hard and fast, cursing Lucien's name even as he imagined those slim fingers doing what he had roughly achieved with his own hand.

He was shaking with reaction, dazed at how vulnerable he felt, ashamed that he hadn't been able to control his own body. Lucien had barely touched him, yet it felt as though a line of fire had seared his skin where that finger had trailed across his flesh.

"What the hell is wrong with me?"

For a few moments he lay staring blankly at the ceiling. He couldn't think straight. Gradually, an awareness of how sticky he was got him off the bed. Ben cleaned himself up and dressed, trying to distract himself with the mundane routine of his morning. He had always been aware of Lucien, though only with a kind of distant admiration. Lord Thorne was so far out of Ben's social sphere that he couldn't imagine ever being friends with him. He could only remember a couple of times when they had spoken. Even then, it had only been because a boat had needed a repair or Lucien had needed something fetching from the equipment store.

Ben had never hidden his own sexuality, though he was hardly vocal about it and he was too shy to approach other men himself. He'd never seen Lucien with a man, but then he'd never seen him with a woman either so that didn't mean anything. He had watched him row and, like everyone else, he had been impressed, but hadn't resorted to the kind of fawning at which Seb was so proficient. After Lucien's regular partner had retired, there had been a great deal of speculation about whom he would choose as a replacement, but then he had started rowing solo and the gossip had died down. Until today. Ben groaned. The entire club would know what had happened by the end of the day and there would be no avoiding the inevitable speculation. Ben hated being in the spotlight. He was much more comfortable staying hidden in the shadows. Now he would have to deal with questions and comments. He couldn't even dismiss the event as a one-off now that Lucien had asked him to row again the next day. Rowers were worse than a bunch of paparazzi when it came to creating a story out of nothing. He resolved to sneak out when he could and hide in the university library for as long as possible.

Chapter Three

Ben had spent the rest of the day in an agony of speculation. Despite his best endeavors, he hadn't been able to get Lucien out of his head. He'd been so distracted that he'd nearly cycled into the river on the way to college, then had spent five minutes sitting in the wrong lecture theater before he'd belatedly realized that he was listening to a professor wax lyrical about microbiology instead of the war poets. He'd met friends for lunch, but had had no idea what they had been talking about until someone had mentioned the auction of promises, which had jerked him abruptly back to reality. It was Thursday and the auction was the following night. An up-and-coming local band had been booked to play and the event was a sell-out. It seemed that his humiliation was going to be very public indeed.

He killed some time in the library, a place he often went if he felt unsettled. There was something about the smell of old books that had a calming effect. He used a single study desk buried deep in the stacks that no one else ever seemed to find. The surrounding shelves were full of massive tomes concerning ancient case law, and from the amount of dust resting on the top of them, it had been years since anyone had needed to use them. Today, however, he still couldn't settle. His concentration was shot to pieces by anxiety about the auction and nervous anticipation of rowing with Lucien again the next day. Ben stared sightlessly at his book and sighed before resting his aching head on his arms. Just how had his life managed to get so bloody complicated?

For the rest of the day he went through the motions. He hardly registered cycling home, making sure everything in the boatshed was in order before the evening crowd arrived, then heading up to his own small apartment to make a sandwich and settle down to some work. Even when he did go to bed, he couldn't sleep properly. Every thirty minutes or so, he would wake from an uneasy doze to look at the clock and check the time. Eventually exhaustion overtook him and he slept more deeply.

* * * *

"Fuck!" Ben woke to the realization that his alarm had failed to go off. It was ten to six. He struggled to extract himself from a tangle of sheets, threw water on his face and grabbed his kit. He was pulling open the boatshed door and cursing the dim light when footsteps crunched on the gravel behind him.

"I would have expected you to be ready by now."

Lucien's tone was stern, edged with impatience. Ben turned to meet a stare that could have frozen the depths of hell. He blinked and lowered his eyes. If he kept looking at that gorgeous face, even more alluring with that smoldering frown, he knew his cock would betray him and he hadn't had time to find a longer top.

"I didn't sleep well…"

"I can tell. You look like crap." Lucien's grin was pure evil as he reached out and ran one finger down Ben's jaw line. "And I'll expect you to have shaved tomorrow."

Ben jerked away from his touch in shock. Even such light contact had sent a thrill straight to his groin, and he hated his involuntary reaction.

"Tomorrow?" His question was colored by indignation that this arrogant bastard had the nerve to criticize stubble at six o'clock in the morning, especially since Lucien's own face was dusted with a dark shadow.

"If you're not too pathetic today."

Jesus. He was unbelievable.

Suppressed fury fueled Ben's rowing that morning, and they shot down the river at an unsustainable speed. At the turn, they idled next to the bank. Ben leaned forward and tried to catch his breath while Lucien relaxed with a satisfied grin.

"I'll have to piss you off more often." His tone was so matter-of-fact that Ben realized instantly that he had fallen for a deliberate ploy to get him worked up.

He snapped back before he could stop himself, "That is unlikely to be a problem."

"So there is some fire behind that meek façade."

Ben didn't look around at Lucien's deep chuckle. The man was fucking infuriating — why did he have to be so unbelievably sexy at the same time? Ben groaned to himself as his errant cock began to swell. He twisted a little in his seat so he could keep half an eye on Lucien.

Lucien's smile betrayed how much he was enjoying himself. Ben could tell that the man thought he was nice and easy to rile. Ben steeled himself and tried to convince his dick that he wasn't enjoying the abuse.

"Take your shirt off."

"What?" Ben twisted fully around to stare at him. "Why?"

"I need to see your muscles working while you row. See how your technique can be improved."

Ben gritted his teeth at the implication that his style would definitely need to be improved. He turned away. "You can see how I move with a shirt on."

"If you were wearing an appropriate top I might agree, but that…thing you have on is far too baggy. Now stop arguing with me and take it off."

Ben gripped the oars tightly and shook his head. He could be stubborn when he wanted to be.

"Do as you're told, Benedict."

Lucien's voice was low, but implied all manner of unpleasant consequences if unquestioning compliance didn't follow.

Ben's stomach twisted and his swollen cock jerked as if it had a life all its own. He found his trembling hands had gripped the hem of his top and yanked it over his head before he'd even realized what he had been doing. He didn't look round. He didn't want to witness the gloating look that he knew would be pasted onto Lucien's handsome features.

The cool breeze brushed his body, turning his nipples into hard, aching nubs, and Ben shivered.

"Better. Now, let's row before you freeze. In future, you'll do as I say immediately."

Lucien maneuvered the boat away from the bank and set his position. Reluctantly, Ben mirrored his actions. Lucien set a slower pace and that gave Ben time to think—something he might have been better off without. It was hard to accept that something inside him responded to being ordered around, but the physical responses he was experiencing couldn't be denied. He sensed Lucien's eyes on his back and wondered what it would feel like to have Lucien's hands on his body. His nipples ached to be touched, sucked and pinched. He could almost feel the exquisitely sharp pain, and had to bite his lip hard to focus his concentration. The thought of getting back to the boathouse and being seen semi-naked poured cold water on his hidden pleasure. Lucien would probably enjoy his humiliation greatly — so he was genuinely surprised when the boat headed toward the bank just before the final bend in the river.

He looked back curiously, just in time to catch Lucien adjusting his shorts to accommodate a sizeable bulge.

"Put your shirt back on."

Relieved, Ben dragged the top over his head. The fabric muffled his hearing so he wasn't sure of Lucien's next words, but he thought he'd heard, "Your body is for my eyes only."

He didn't have time to contemplate what that might've meant as they reached the boathouse and disembarked. Neither man spoke while they carried the boat along the path. They stowed it securely, than racked the oars. Ben found his gaze constantly drawn to Lucien's arse, to his perfectly tapered torso, concealed only by clinging black fabric.

Lucien assessed him coolly. "Shower. Now."

Ben found himself meekly following Lucien into the deserted changing room, rather than heading upstairs to the relative safety of his own flat.

Lucien gave him a knowing smile and stripped off his rowing kit without any hesitation before strolling into the first shower cubicle. He had an amazingly toned body and moved with an unselfconscious, graceful power. Ben followed more slowly, taking the stall next to him, hiding beneath the steaming spray. He felt jittery and nervous, so he put all his concentration into soaping himself down. The sight of Lucien's nakedness had done things to his body that needed to be dealt with. He inevitably wrapped his hand around his stiff, slippery cock, but froze when he felt a presence behind him.

Lucien didn't speak, but wrapped one strong arm around Ben's chest and pulled him back, so that their bodies were locked together.

"What are you doing?"

Ben didn't want or expect an answer to his whispered question, and he didn't get one. He couldn't move. He dropped his hand slackly to his side. He wanted to pull away. He wanted to press even closer. He felt sick and dizzy as Lucien bit into the soft flesh of his neck, then sucked viciously, marking him. His legs wobbled and his balls ached as Lucien's other arm tightly encircled his waist. Lucien stroked his stomach and chest. Ben could feel a rock-hard cock lodged into the valley between his arse cheeks, probing lightly at his entrance. Then, just as he had imagined earlier, Lucien gave his nipples a cruel twist.

With an indignant gasp, Ben came hard. Lucien held him firmly, pinning his arms so that Ben couldn't touch himself, and rubbed up and down against his arse. Ben felt slick warmth slide down his thigh as Lucien ejaculated with a satisfied sigh. Then soft, warm lips were against his ear, whispering words he could hardly hear through the noisy pounding of blood racing through his veins.

"You did quite well today. Room for improvement, though. I'll see you at six tomorrow — and make sure you have a fucking shave."

With one strong hand, he gave Ben's softening dick a less than gentle tug, and the thought flashed through Ben's mind that shaving his face wasn't Lucien's only requirement. Then the light brightened and the presence behind him was gone.

Ben leaned against the cubicle wall and shook. Why hadn't he resisted? He pressed a hand against his neck, rubbing at the bruise he knew would be appearing there. Lucien had marked him and it felt right. It was all so confusing. He felt utterly drained, literally and figuratively, and the day was only just beginning.

Chapter Four

Every time Ben closed his eyes he imagined Lucien's hard body pressed against him. The sensations were all pervasive and it was impossible to concentrate. His imagination tortured him further with images of what might have happened if Lucien hadn't left. His nipples ached and a livid bruise had appeared at the soft juncture of his neck and shoulder. Ben shuddered involuntarily. He liked a little pain, and it seemed that Lucien enjoyed delivering it. He could still feel that restrictive arm around him and knew instinctively that restraint, rather than affection, had been Lucien's objective. Ben had felt helplessly overpowered and it had been wonderful.

In the end, he threw on some old sweats and went for a long run along the riverbank. He pushed himself hard until the demands of his body took all his focus. He got back to the boathouse soaked in sweat, limbs trembling from exertion, but at least he was more in control of his emotions. Control was one thing—but it didn't take away his underlying sense of nervous excitement, or the vague irritation that one man could have such a dramatic impact on him in such a short time.

It was early afternoon and there were only a couple of boats out on the water. There was no one around so he took a quick shower in the changing rooms, then put on a pair of old jeans, ripped across one thigh but too comfortable to throw away, and a navy T-shirt that had been a present from his mother. It had a designer label that he couldn't afford for himself, and it hugged his shape nicely. Still warm from his run, he didn't bother with a sweater and padded around the flat in bare feet.

After a quick lunch, he settled down to study. He had no need to go into university and he wanted to avoid being anywhere near the auction of promises, which would be held in one of the university's function rooms. It was going to be a black tie affair, and the tickets had cost a fortune. The concept that people would pay money so that they could spend more money was beyond him, but he realized that the event was mostly about appearances. He was thankful that he didn't have to show up in person.

The lots had been advertised for a while, so there would be no bidding on the night. Anyone interested in a lot had submitted a sealed bid, which protected the identities of those who had bid too low. The winners would be announced on the night in between dinner and entertainment. His own promise had been added late, so he was sure it wouldn't attract much interest. Seb would no doubt take great pleasure in letting him know how little he had been 'sold' for.

A wry chuckle escaped him. Let Seb have his moment—Ben really didn't care. He got back to his essay and actually managed to write a few passable paragraphs before the phone rang. Ben picked it up and immediately wished he hadn't.

"Astor, good, you're there."

Ben groaned silently. "Seb. What can I do for you?"

"Glad you asked. My barman for the auction tonight has cried off—some lame excuse about his brother having a motorbike accident. I need you here by seven."

"No! I'm not going anywhere near that place. You don't own me, Seb—and, anyway, I'm working here tonight."

"No, you're not. I've given the spare keys to Gabe. He'll close up. You can clear up tomorrow morning. That means you owe me three hours, so get your arse over here on time."

Ben felt like beating his head against the desk. "The auction will take more than three hours." His defense was desperate and he knew he was fighting a losing battle.

"Yes, it will, which is good because you need to earn some time off so you can fulfill your own promise. I have to find someone to cover your lazy arse while you do your twenty-four-hour stint, so quit fucking complaining and be here."

The connection clicked and Ben was left with the dial tone droning in his ear. He leaned back in his chair and stared at the ceiling.

"Fuck."

That just about summed it up. The auction wasn't due to finish until midnight—he'd have to clear up and cycle home, which meant he was unlikely to get to bed before two. He then had to be up and ready for Lucien at six, and the man didn't exactly exude patience and understanding. At twenty-one, Ben was a little past the age where an afternoon nap was a possibility. The tension built in his neck and shoulders and he tried to relax, but it was too late to stop the nagging headache behind his eyes. He threw himself back into his work, confining all thoughts of the auction to a small area of his mind marked 'don't go there'. After a couple of hours, the persistent headache threatened to become a migraine. Ben took a bottle of water from the fridge and swallowed a couple of extra-strength paracetamol. No way did he want to tend a noisy bar feeling any worse than he already did. He rested on his bed until the pounding in his head receded a bit then got up to change his clothes.

Unsure what to wear, not having received any instructions from Seb, he eventually decided on black trousers and an Okeanos polo shirt. The top was dark green with a silver logo—nothing to make him stand out, which was exactly what he wanted. If he had to be there, he wanted to be as anonymous as possible. He shuddered at the thought of all those eyes on him when the bidding on his promise was announced. The knot in his stomach tightened—what if there had been no bids at all? His cheeks warmed at the thought of the potential humiliation. He had to splash cold water on his face and give himself a good mental talking to before he could summon up the courage to leave.

When Ben got to the venue, Seb was waiting and already doing his best to give himself an ulcer, yelling orders at a range of harried staff and volunteers. Ben wheeled his bike into the back of the cloakroom and locked it up before facing Seb's sarcasm. Fortunately, Seb was too worried about the event to do more than communicate a few instructions about the bar stock and how to operate the cash register.

"All you have to deal with is wine, beer and soft drinks. If they want anything else they'll have to go to the uni bar. It's cash only—don't accept any checks. There's a float in the till so you should be okay for change. The table wine is included with the ticket price, so you shouldn't be too busy during the meal. And for Christ's sake, try to look a bit happier—people have paid good money to be here tonight and they don't need you looking like your pet hamster just had a coronary on its fucking wheel."

He was already walking off to do something else.

"Wait. Who else is coming to help?" Ben called after him as he eyed the precarious stacks of crates and barrels warily.

Seb laughed unpleasantly. "You might actually have to work tonight, Astor. You're on your own. I suggest you visit the john now, because once we get going you're not to move from behind that bar. Understand? Don't drink too much or I might just have to tie a knot in it. Not that that wouldn't be fun."

Ben opened his mouth to protest, but Seb was already turning away. Bastard.

Half an hour of shifting things around to get them more organized was followed by a frantic hour of serving drinks before two hundred people sat down for dinner. Ben poured himself a glass of water and drank deeply—even the threat to his innocent dick was not enough to stop him draining the glass with relief. He felt disgusting, hot and sticky, and his arms were scratched and sore from wrenching open boxes and heaving barrels around.

He leaned against the bar and, for the first time, got the chance to look around at the diners. Since they were done up in their dinner jackets, he hardly recognized some of his rowing friends. The girls were dressed in every variation of evening dress from short and sparkly to long and formal. He amused himself for a while by giving points out of ten to some of the hotter guys—not that he would ever dare approach any of them, but it was fun. He caught sight of Seb, holding court near the front of the room, his braying laugh clearly audible above the general din of conversation. The guy was in his element, but still managed to look like a complete arse.

A tap on the bar pulled his attention back to what he was supposed to be doing.

"Hey, blondie, anybody home?"

Ben smiled sheepishly. "Sorry, I was daydreaming. What can I do for you?"

He blushed as he realized the guy in front of him was shamelessly looking him up and down with a somewhat predatory grin.

"Hi, I'm Zac. I'm with the band. Can you open the fire doors so we can get our kit in?"

Ben nodded, taking in black, spiky hair and deep brown eyes circled with black eyeliner. Zac was cute in a scary kind of way.

"You're late. You'll have to move quickly to get set up."

"Yeah, the piece of shit van we use broke down on the way here. Third time this week. Still, the RAC guy was hot." Zac's lopsided grin was disarming.

Ben took him out to the back corridor and tried to ignore the black leather cupping Zac's nicely curved arse.

"Sorry I can't help bring the kit in—I have to watch the bar."

"No problem. There are four of us. We can manage fine. Perhaps I could come by for a drink later, after we've done our set?"

Ben bit his lip and managed a shy smile. "Sure, that would be nice."

Zac chuckled and wiggled his hips shamelessly as he walked away. Ben enjoyed the outrageous flirting.

Maybe the evening wouldn't be quite so horrible after all.

Chapter Five

The auction announcements went without a hitch and Ben was amazed at the amount of money some people had bid for the lots. Two hundred quid for a Harrods picnic on the river, over a thousand for a weekend in a lighthouse on the coast. His own promise had been tacked onto the end of the list and he was serving a rowdy bunch of half-drunk rowers when the winning bid was read out. There was a collective gasp from the audience and two hundred faces turned toward the bar. One of the young men waiting for a drink leaned toward the nearest table and asked what was going on.

"Five grand. Someone bid five grand for Ben's promise!"

Ben blanched. "What? Who?" This was worse than no bids at all.

"Anonymous bidder."

There was a rustle and fidgeting as an envelope was passed from table to table until it finally reached Ben's shaking hands. On the microphone, Seb could barely conceal the envy in his voice. "The envelope contains instructions for fulfilling the promise."

He immediately went on to some more announcements about the total raised, and people rapidly lost interest in Ben's embarrassment and went back to their conversations. The band started their set and gradually the dance floor filled. Ben was left alone with his envelope.

For a while he ignored it and watched the band. Zac was playing bass guitar and looked suitably cool. The lead singer was a bald, tattooed guy with a voice like melted chocolate. He held the microphone close enough to kiss. The group covered a range of soft rock tunes and threw in a couple of their own—it was a pretty good sound and they were getting an enthusiastic reception from the crowd. Ben looked forward to talking to Zac when they were done.

He fingered the envelope. It was high quality paper, thick and creamy. On the outside in black ink were the words *Promise 50, instructions*. That was it. He slid a finger beneath the flap and eased out a single, folded sheet of paper. Nervously he opened it, but frowned when he read the single line written on the paper.

Sunday, 8 a.m. Mortimer's Crossroads.

Ben shrugged. It was all very mysterious but he didn't have time to worry about it. People were starting to filter back from the dance floor, wanting more drinks. He tucked the piece of paper into his pocket and got back to work.

Midnight came and went, and a well-lubricated crowd headed for home. The band packed up amps and instruments, then gathered round the bar for a drink. Ben was beginning to feel a bit shaky—he hadn't eaten since lunchtime and it had been a long, hard night. He poured himself an orange juice and listened to the band talking about their next gig. He didn't miss the fact that Zac was continually glancing in his direction but, though it was flattering, it felt wrong to be interested. He didn't know why he felt that way. He was single. Zac was attractive and definitely into him. What was the problem?

To mask his own confusion, Ben began to clear tables, stacking glasses on the bar and filling crates with empty bottles. The band headed out to their van but Zac lingered, a small smile playing around his lips.

"So, is it worth me waiting around for you to finish?"

Ben's face heated and he lowered his eyes, not knowing what to say.

"No. It's not."

Ben jumped as Lucien's pissed off voice answered for him. A hand rested on the back of his neck and squeezed gently.

Zac scowled but took a couple of steps back. "Sorry. I didn't realize he was taken."

"I'm not—"

"No problem." Lucien's tone was totally dismissive and Zac took the hint with a disappointed sigh. As he disappeared outside, Ben extracted himself from Lucien's grip and turned to face him. His intent had been to protest at being treated like a piece of property but when he took in the tall, dark figure in front of him, dressed in a dinner jacket, his bow tie undone and hanging loosely around his neck, he froze. Fuck, the man was gorgeous. For a few seconds he just stared, then suddenly found his tongue and his self-respect.

"What the hell, Lucien? What right do you have to—?"

Lucien ignored him. "I'll help you finish up here and then I'll take you home."

"I can get myself home, thanks."

Ben retreated from Lucien's glare until the bar pressed into his back. Lucien followed with deliberate steps until he was just a few inches away. He shook his head slowly, "Don't argue with me, Benedict. It will get you precisely nowhere."

Then he gripped Ben's hair and pulled him forward into a crushing kiss. Ben tried to resist but Lucien pushed his tongue against him, breaching his lips to explore at will. Ben found his own arms circling Lucien's neck, pulling him closer, deeper. The intensity of their contact set his cock on fire. He couldn't think, couldn't breathe... Suddenly there was cool air in his lungs as Lucien released him and took a step back with a knowing smirk. Then he walked off and began to clear tables as if nothing had happened.

Ben watched for a while in disbelief, chewing on his already swollen lower lip. Once again he had surrendered himself to this arrogant, presumptuous son of a bitch — and, he admitted to himself, had loved every second. Where the hell had Lucien come from, anyway? He hadn't been at the auction. Ben went back to stacking glasses with shaking hands until everything was cleared.

Lucien strolled to the door and looked back at him expectantly. "Let's go."

Ben thought about arguing for all of ten seconds, then followed him out to the car park.

"My bike is...not going to fit in that."

Lights flashed as Lucien unlocked his low, sleek Aston Martin and Ben tried not to drool.

"You can collect it tomorrow. Get in."

Too tired to argue, Ben sank into butter-soft leather and enjoyed the luxury. The walnut dashboard gleamed. Polished chrome instruments glinted in the low light. The whole interior was a work of art. Ben stroked a wooden door panel and breathed in the scent of leather.

"If you're going to orgasm over my car, there are wipes in the glovebox," Lucien said, his tone full of amusement.

Ben was so tired, he wasn't sure if he was awake or dreaming. He heard the roar of the engine firing up. The low rumble soothed him. His eyes drifted closed and even Lucien's close proximity wasn't enough to keep him awake.

* * * *

"Ben. Wake up." Lucien gently shook his shoulder. Ben's stomach growled and he moaned as his eyes flickered open.

"Wake up. You're too heavy to carry!"

"Are you saying I'm fat?" Ben mumbled the words before he was fully awake.

Blue eyes narrowed. "Jesus. You're completely out of it, aren't you?"

Lucien slammed his door shut and circled the car to hold Ben's open. Slightly more awake, Ben struggled out and groped for his keys. Impatiently, Lucien thrust a hand into one of his pockets and felt around. He grinned as Ben jerked beneath his touch, then pulled out Ben's key ring and handed it to him. "Relax. You're exhausted, starving and you're filthy. I have no intention of taking advantage of you…tonight. Eat something. Go to bed. I'll see you in the morning."

He guided Ben toward his door. "And, Ben…"

"I know, I know. I'll have a bloody shave."

Lucien smirked. "I was going to say make sure you get up early enough to eat something."

Ben was skeptical and it must have shown on his face.

"Then I was going to mention the shaving."

Ben rolled his eyes. "I can't eat before I row with you, I'll only throw up."

"My company turns your stomach that badly, does it?"

"Humor really doesn't suit you," Ben said. "If you've done tormenting me, I'd like to use the next four precious hours for sleep."

Lucien cupped the nape of his neck and pulled him close. The kiss that followed was surprisingly gentle, if inescapable.

"Sleep well." Lucien walked back toward his car, and Ben was left wondering if he'd just experienced an exhaustion-induced hallucination.

Chapter Six

Four hours of sleep did little for Ben's mood the next morning. He shocked himself awake with a cold shower, shaved carefully then stared at himself in the mirror. Pale gray eyes stared accusingly back.

"Pathetic. You should have grown a beard just to annoy him."

He ran a finger across his jaw, then looked tentatively down at his newly smooth groin. He actually liked the way it looked, though it made him feel young and vulnerable. What he didn't like was the strange feeling that he had somehow been compelled to apply the razor down there.

Lucien was sending very strong signals, but Ben still wasn't sure whether the man actually liked him or whether he was just amusing himself. He sighed. If only he wasn't so... God, he didn't even know how to describe just how enthralling he found Lucien. His brain told him to run, but he was so turned on by such unrestrained dominance that he knew, deep down, that he was going nowhere.

He scrubbed his teeth, pulled on some clothes and ran downstairs to unlock the boatshed. He'd finished getting everything ready and a few people were already arriving so he found a quiet spot to stretch his stiff muscles and warm himself up a bit. He was so absorbed in what he was doing that he didn't notice Lucien until a hand rested on his arse and patted firmly.

Ben nearly fell over at Lucien's low chuckle. "Bending over like that in front of me could get you into deep trouble."

For a fleeting moment, Ben wondered how deep—he was already completely out of his depth where Lucien was concerned. He turned so he was facing Lucien's gaze and allowed his eyes to wander across his hard body, attractively encased in the usual black Lycra. His stare lingered on the impressive bulge in a pair of very tight shorts and he decided that any more stretching would have to wait.

"Put this on."

Automatically, Ben reached up to catch the garment that had been thrown at him. It was a very expensive-looking navy blue rowing top, with narrow white panels down the sides.

"What's wrong with my shirt?"

Lucien snarled, "What's right with it? Put that on or row shirtless, the choice is yours, but I am not getting in a boat with you while you're wearing that rag. That's an old one of mine, you can keep it."

Knowing that the top had once been wrapped around Lucien's muscular form made all the difference. Ben pulled off his baggy T-shirt, put on Lucien's top and tried to get accustomed to the feel of fabric hugging him much more closely than he was used to.

Lucien was scowling, as usual, though there was a hint of a smile behind the grumpiness. Ben felt so self-conscious. The dark garment displayed his body much more blatantly. It was so tight there was no hiding anything. The way he looked seemed to be having an effect on Lucien too. Ben just caught sight of the prominent bulge in his shorts before Lucien set off toward the river. Ben hummed to himself as he followed, secretly glad that he could do things to affect that amazing body.

They rowed hard, and for longer than usual. Even Lucien looked tired by the time they got back. Ben was nervously excited as they headed for the showers, but the changing rooms were crowded and there was no way there was going to be a repeat of the previous day.

By the time they had finished dressing, they were alone. In jeans and a pale blue shirt, Lucien looked more relaxed than usual. His dark hair was damp and tousled and Ben wanted nothing more than to run his fingers through it. Lucien, of course, caught him staring. The man seemed to have a sixth sense when it came to catching Ben's secretive glances.

"Tomorrow, then."

"I can't." Ben felt flustered. "I have to fulfill my promise from the auction last night. I won't have time to row first."

"Of course. Someone paid a lot of money for you, didn't they?"

The way he'd said it made it sound like Ben had sold his body rather than his labor.

"You weren't at the auction—I would have seen you. How did you know I was there last night? Where did you come from?"

"I'm not standing here in the men's locker room discussing my social life. If you want to talk, you can make me breakfast."

Ben blinked uncertainly. "Uh…okay." Christ, he sounded like a tongue-tied idiot.

He was painfully aware of how close Lucien was behind him as they climbed the stairs to his small apartment. In his mind, Ben ran through the contents of the fridge, thankful that he had found the time to do some shopping earlier in the week.

Lucien threw himself into one of the two old armchairs and stretched out his long legs, casting a critical glance around the small apartment.

"This place isn't too bad, is it?"

"It's warm and it's free. That's good enough as far as I'm concerned." Ben followed Lucien's gaze. "The only downside is having to do what Seb tells me to."

Lucien chuckled. "Seb has unresolved issues. He likes to take his frustration out on someone and at the moment, you're it. Take it as a compliment. If you were short, fat and ugly, he wouldn't give you the time of day."

"It doesn't feel complimentary when I'm on my knees scrubbing out the Gents."

Lucien's expression changed slightly. "Please don't present me with images of you on your knees when I have an empty stomach." His eyes glinted hungrily, but his growing appetite obviously had nothing to do with food.

Ben shifted nervously and hid behind the kitchen counter. He opened the fridge and shoved his burning face into the cool air. "Do you want healthy or cholesterol killer? I can do muesli, porridge or bacon and eggs."

He stood up and nearly jumped out of his skin as Lucien wrapped his arms around Ben from behind. Soothingly, he stroked Ben's hair. "Shh. Relax. You don't have to be frightened of me."

Ben trembled and despite Lucien's words he was terrified, though his fear was more to do with his own desires than the man holding him so tightly.

His voice was little more than a whisper. "What do you want from me, Lucien? Please don't play with me."

He felt Lucien's body stiffen, then Lucien gently planted kisses on Ben's neck.

"I don't play, Benedict. Believe me, I'm deadly serious when it comes to you."

Ben tested Lucien's hold, but he was being firmly restrained.

"You hardly know me."

Lucien nibbled one of his earlobes and Ben's cock jumped. He made a half-hearted attempt to get free, but Lucien clearly had no intention of letting him go.

"I've been watching you for six months. I think you'd be surprised as to how much I do know about you."

Ben pressed back against him in surprise. "Six months? Are you some kind of mad stalker?"

Lucien found his neck and sucked viciously on the half-healed bruise that he had put there before. Ben gasped at the sudden pain, but his swollen dick twitched with excitement.

"Like that, don't you?"

Lucien pushed strands of hair away and dug his teeth into soft flesh. He didn't bite hard enough to break the skin, but it was painful. Ben squirmed against him but made no real attempt to escape.

He did the unexpected and let go.

"Sit down. I'll cook."

Ben took a few faltering steps toward the chair and sat down. "I can only take so many shocks in one day, Lucien. You cooking may just be the final straw."

Lucien scowled and dropped rashers of bacon into a pan. "You're treading on dangerous ground, Benedict."

He flipped the rashers expertly. "I started watching you when I needed to look for a new rowing partner. You lack discipline, but you have talent — a natural flair. The more I watched, the more I liked what I saw, and I'm not just talking about your skill with a set of oars."

"I thought you decided to take up single sculling after Ed retired?"

"I prefer pairs. I needed to find out if I could row with you without being too distracted."

Eggs sizzled and the room filled with enticing aromas. Lucien slammed bread into the toaster with unnecessary force.

"I don't understand..." Ben felt a little dizzy. He needed to eat. Lucien gestured to a plate on the counter and Ben pulled up a stool.

"I don't just want to row with you, Ben."

Not knowing what to say, Ben took a forkful of eggs and chewed on some toast. Slowly, he gathered his courage and raised his eyes. Lucien stared at him with unconcealed lust, the soft blue of his eyes shot through with fire. Deliberately Ben placed his fork across his plate. "So...what do you want?"

Lucien looked uncertain for a fraction of a second, but he met Ben's gaze and smiled.

"I want you to be mine." He stood and took one of Ben's hands into his own, playing gently with his fingers and rubbing a thumb across his palm. Then the gentleness was replaced by something else and he gripped Ben's slim wrist tightly, squeezing enough to hurt.

Ben flinched, but didn't try to pull away. He could barely breathe, his cock was on fire and he had no words to voice his understanding of Lucien's need.

"I want your obedience. I want to punish you when you disobey. You so much as glance at another man with those beautiful eyes and I'll... Never mind what I'll do. Just don't test me."

Lucien reached down to rub Ben's aching erection through his jeans. "You don't seem to be averse to this arrangement?" He paused. "I'm not a monster, Ben. You have to want this too. I'll never hurt you more than you can take. I'll never do anything you don't agree to."

He exerted a little more pressure on Ben's wrist and continued to rub his other hand up and down. Ben tried desperately to control his body, but it was no good. The heat of his orgasm fired into his underwear as his cock spasmed again and again.

With a strangled cry, he wrenched himself free and ran for the shower, not daring to look back.

In the bathroom, Ben cleaned himself up and retrieved semi-clean clothes from the laundry hamper. Looking scruffy was one hundred percent preferable to walking out there naked from the waist down. He wanted to laugh and cry at the same time. The most gorgeous man he'd ever met wanted him. *Him!* But Lucien wanted so much more than a simple relationship.

"I should have known this wouldn't be easy..." Ben muttered at the mirror. "I couldn't meet a nice, uncomplicated guy, could I? Oh, no..."

He pushed open the door and walked across to the kitchen. He could feel Lucien's gaze on him as he boiled the kettle and made two mugs of coffee—it was making the hairs on the back of his neck stand on end.

He held a mug out to Lucien and was proud of the fact that his hand didn't shake too much.

"You are very pretty when you're flustered."

All of Ben's composure disappeared in an instant.

Lucien's smile was devilish—he knew exactly what he was doing, keeping Ben off balance. "Christ, Lucien, are you trying to emasculate me completely? You're hard enough to cope with as it is."

Lucien smiled and sipped his coffee slowly. To Ben's relief, he remained silent while Ben worked up the courage to say what was on his mind. Ben remained standing. He didn't feel as if he should sit down without permission—ridiculous in his own home, but that was how he felt.

"I like you, Lucien. A lot, despite the fact that you intimidate the hell out of me. But I'm not sure I can do what you ask." His voice faltered and he hung his head.

Lucien was undeterred. "Because you don't want to be with me?"

"No! No, that's not it. Who wouldn't want to be with you? But you ask a lot..."

"I freely admit to being demanding. You'll get used to it."

"I can't just agree to this here and now. Give me some time..."

Lucien put his mug down and stood up. "You have to fulfill your promise tomorrow, which will be done with by eight on Monday morning. Will your classes allow you to row late—say ten o'clock?"

Ben nodded.

"Fine. I'll see you then."

Before Ben knew what was happening he was being thoroughly kissed. Stubble raked his cheek and Lucien nipped at his lip. He cupped Ben's arse and pulled him close.

"I know you want this, Ben—you just have to admit it to yourself. I was certain as soon as I saw you'd shaved for me."

"You saw? Oh God." Ben thought he might die of humiliation.

"You anticipated what I wanted. That in itself is just as hot as the end result." Lucien sauntered across to the door. "Enjoy tomorrow."

Then he was gone. Ben collapsed into the chair Lucien had just vacated and breathed in his scent. He already knew that he was going to do exactly what Lucien wanted — the man was irresistible — but this delay felt like he was at least managing to assert some independence. Lucien wasn't going to get everything his own way.

Chapter Seven

At a quarter to eight the next morning, Mortimer's Crossroads were shrouded in mist. A heavy frost lay on the grass and Ben was glad that he'd worn a thick fleece over his jeans. He pulled his gloves on tighter and rewound the scarf around his neck, stamping his feet to keep warm. He was a bit early for his mysterious rendezvous, but his travel options were limited and the only bus to the nearest village had dropped him off at half past. He hadn't wanted to cycle, not knowing how he was to be collected.

The narrow country lanes were edged with woodland and the light was still dim. In the distance a fox crossed the road and stopped to give him a curious glance, then shot into the trees as a car approached. Ben was a little nervous but his thoughts were on Lucien—a big enough distraction to keep his mind away from what the mystery bidder might want to do with him.

The approaching car pulled over and the window slid down.

"Hi. Are you Ben?"

The young woman peering out of the window had to be about twenty-eight, naturally pretty with little makeup. She smiled encouragingly.

"Yes. That's me."

"Well. I can see what all the fuss was about. Get in. You must be freezing."

Gratefully, Ben climbed into the warm interior of the car and pulled the door shut. "So, are you the generous bidder that won me?" He was relieved — the woman looked nice so perhaps the day wouldn't be too arduous.

"Sorry, no. Though now I've seen you, I could certainly think of a few things to do with you!" She chuckled at his embarrassment. "I'm just the chauffeur."

"So who was the bidder then?"

"Not allowed to tell you, I'm afraid. Very strict instructions, more than my life's worth, et cetera, et cetera." She accelerated smoothly down the empty road. "Don't look so worried — it won't be all bad."

"Oh, God. You are so not helping..." Ben's imagination was running wild. 'Not all bad' meant 'not all good'. Fuck, what had Seb got him into? He resolved to tell the man exactly what he thought of him when all this was over. Twenty-four hours suddenly seemed like a very long time.

"I'm Madeleine, Maddy to my friends. We don't have far to go."

She drove along narrow, winding roads for about ten minutes, then turned in through some open gates next to a small lodge. Ben couldn't see a sign or a nameplate, but the drive turned a corner through the trees, and a large, gothic mansion came into view. Hundreds of panes of glass caught the light, making the building sparkle. Acres of parkland bordered a landscaped formal garden and a lake that looked natural but probably wasn't. Ben could just picture a wet-shirted Mr. Darcy wading from the water.

"It's beautiful." Ben looked at the house with genuine admiration.

"Thanks. It is, rather, isn't it? Costs a bloody fortune to maintain, though, and try finding a window cleaner who's prepared to run a squeegee over that lot."

"Is it yours, then?" Ben felt a little envious, but Maddy laughed.

"No. Let's just say it's in the family. I'm sure you'll find out more about the place later."

Maddy wound the car between some outbuildings and came to a halt outside an old stable block. Several horses twitched their ears in Ben's direction as he got out of the car and looked around. He put his small overnight bag on the stone mounting block against one wall and watched as Maddy turned the car around, switched off the ignition and walked over.

"You have to put this on."

She held out a length of black cloth and Ben raised his eyebrows.

"What is it?"

"Oh, you really are an innocent, aren't you?" She laughed at his confused expression. "It's a blindfold."

Ben's lips formed an 'oh', but no sound came out.

"Turn around. I can't believe I'm doing this..." Maddy reached up and fastened the strip of cloth around his eyes, then guided him back to sit on the mounting block next to his bag. "If it wasn't for the trade-off..."

Blind and feeling more than a little anxious Ben asked, "What do you mean, trade-off?"

A hand touched his shoulder. "The only reason I'm doing this is because I'm now owed three nights of babysitting. I have six-year-old twin boys so that is an excellent bargain—you have no idea!"

Despite his situation, Ben managed a laugh. "So, what now?"

"Well, you stay put. Something tells me you won't have to wait long. It was nice to meet you, Ben."

Footsteps crunched across the gravel before the car started up and pulled off.

Once the sound had died away, Ben listened hard for any indication that someone was near. He was very tempted to take the blindfold off but resisted the urge. He shivered a little at the thought that someone might be watching him, and hoped that his mystery buyer wouldn't take too long to reveal his or her presence.

The brush of air against his face was the only thing that betrayed movement and someone's approach. Ben flinched as fingers pulled at the tie of his blindfold and it dropped away. His eyes adjusted to the now bright morning light, and he focused on the figure in front of him, before he scrubbed a trembling hand through his hair. His stomach flipped over.

"I should have bloody known..."

Chapter Eight

Ben looked up into Lucien's eyes, acknowledged the amusement that seemed to make the soft blue glitter, and sighed.

"I am so dumb."

"Did you really think that I would allow you to spend twenty-four hours alone with a stranger? Possibly another man?" Lucien shook his dark head in exaggerated disbelief. "That was never going to happen."

He picked up the blindfold from where it had fallen across Ben's thigh and wound it deliberately around his own hand.

"*Allow?* You really are an arrogant son of a bitch, aren't you?" Ben got to his feet and met Lucien's narrowed eyes with a confidence he didn't feel. "Did you set this up from the start?"

"That's something you'll have to wonder about, now, isn't it? But for the next twenty-four hours, Benedict, you're mine to do with as I choose. Unless you want to back out?"

Ben shuffled his feet nervously. "What exactly do you want me to do?"

Lucien gave a short laugh. "That would be telling. I'm giving you a chance to turn around and go home. I won't withdraw the money whatever you decide, so you don't have to feel obligated. If you stay, you do so willingly."

He twisted his slim fingers into Ben's hair and pulled his head forwards. "But if you stay, you'll do exactly as I say for the next twenty-four hours."

The kiss that followed was savagely sweet, and Ben found himself responding as if it was the most natural thing in the world. He forced himself to disconnect his brain from his dick and pulled away with a gasp.

"You are unbelievable!" He paced up and down, ignoring the twitch of amusement at the corner of Lucien's mouth. "The money is irrelevant. I made a promise—I intend to keep it."

"The promise was forced on you, Ben. I'm fully aware that Seb hijacked you. I don't want to keep you here under some false sense of honor." Lucien snapped the words out impatiently. "Just admit that you want to stay."

Ben froze. It was as if the man could read his mind and he felt like he'd been caught out. He did want to stay. It was a chance to learn more about Lucien Thorne and he needed to understand why he was so drawn to him, but it felt dangerous. Showing any weakness to Lucien was a huge risk, but maybe it was time to be brave and follow his feelings.

He felt anything but brave as he whispered the words that Lucien wanted to hear. "I want to stay."

"There, that wasn't so hard now, was it?"

If there was a way to sound more patronizing, Ben was damn sure he didn't know about it. What the hell was he getting himself into? He focused on jet-black hair and chiseled features and felt himself melting inside. Surely anyone that looked this good had to have some redeeming qualities? It was just a matter of finding them.

"Are you going to stand there all day?" Lucien turned and walked toward the house. Ben tried not to think about how he would have looked to Lucien as he'd waited for him, blindfolded and vulnerable. He was a bundle of nerves and he hoped that Lucien's obvious need to dominate came with a healthy dose of protectiveness.

Agreeing to stay had brought with it a feeling of relief that was almost overwhelming. He'd found the courage to make a decision and it was liberating. Lucien didn't seem to want to let him out of his sight for a moment and Ben felt like he was balancing on a very fine line—it wouldn't take much to frighten him away, but now he had gifted Lucien with twenty-four hours to convince Ben that this was what he wanted.

He watched nervously as Lucien fingered the roll of black cloth in his pocket and felt the slow burn begin to build in his cock. Ben was pretty certain that it wouldn't be long before the blindfold was used again, but next time he knew he wouldn't get away so lightly.

When Ben caught up with Lucien, he had regained his composure and resolved to stop acting like such a wuss. He could meet the conditions of his promise without turning into a doormat. He kept pace with Lucien's long strides and took a proper look at the imposing house.

"So, who was the woman that picked me up?"

Lucien slowed down a little. "Maddy's my sister."

"She was nice…" Ben swallowed, realizing that his tone had implied some doubt that she could therefore be related to Lucien.

Lucien gave a low chuckle. "Somehow, I don't think you would be quite so attracted to me if I were 'nice', Ben. And you are attracted to me, aren't you? You like my hands on your body, my lips against yours… You've certainly done nothing to stop me so far."

"You haven't given me much choice!" Ben used his indignation to hide his unvoiced agreement.

"True. And you like that too."

Ben rolled his eyes. Getting into an argument with Lucien was going to go nowhere so he changed the subject.

"Maddy said the house wasn't hers but that it was in the family. Is it yours?"

"Yes. My father was a traditionalist. I inherited everything on his death. Maddy got nothing."

"So… You live here?"

"No. Maddy does." Ben was confused and it must have been obvious, because Lucien explained. "I live in the old gamekeeper's house on the estate. Maddy and her family live in the main house — well, part of it. Most of it is rented out for filming. We don't open to the public, apart from occasional private tours, but the place has to earn its keep. Fortunately, the house and grounds are in demand for everything from feature films to advertising shoots. Maddy runs the business and her husband James runs the farming side of things. You'd like him — he's 'nice' too. They also have twin boys. The pair of them have the combined energy rating of a small nuclear power station."

"That explains how pleased she was about the babysitting…"

"She told you! Fuck."

"And you gave up your inheritance to them when you could have been lording it over them in the big house."

Lucien shrugged. "They need the space a lot more than I do."

Ben smiled to himself. Lucien clearly had a soft spot for his sister and his nephews, however much he tried to hide it. Perhaps Ben had just discovered the first chink in Lucien's armor and there was a warm heart beating beneath the ice.

"I'll give you a tour of the house this evening, but we've got work to do first and you need to change into something more practical."

"*We've* got work to do? Are you not going to make me slave for you while you supervise and give orders?"

"Oh don't worry—I'll be giving you plenty of orders. Something I know you enjoy as much as you try to hide it."

Lucien led Ben through a small side door and along a cold stone corridor to a storeroom. Inside, there were overalls hanging on pegs alongside waxed coats, and an array of boots were neatly lined up against the wall. Lucien rummaged around and handed Ben a set of the overalls.

"You are going to get hot and dirty…" Ben took a nervous step back at that, and Lucien smirked. "Not with me—well, not just yet, anyway. Take off anything you don't want ruined and put these on. Find yourself some boots that fit." He proceeded to strip off his jumper and T-shirt before pulling the protective clothing on over his jeans. He let the top part hang around his waist and glared at Ben, who was transfixed by the sight of his smooth, muscular torso. "You know, you're not doing a great job of hiding your feelings…"

Ben gave a start and flushed before pulling off his fleece and donning work gear too. Caught again. Now Lucien was going to make his life hell.

* * * *

Mucking out the stables proved to be hot and dirty work, exactly as Lucien had described. Ben forked tons of hay, wheeled barrow-loads of manure, hosed and brushed down the yard. It was back-breaking work, and he was sweating profusely by the time everything was finished. Lucien had taken great delight in ordering him around, but had worked just as hard. Every now and then, Ben had caught him patting a horse or muttering into a velvety ear. They had been joined by three boisterous Labradors who'd played around their feet and had generally got in the way until Lucien had ordered them to lie down, which they all had, instantly.

He glanced across at Ben. "You should take note. That's what obedience looks like."

Ben's eyes widened. He was about to snap back a sarcastic retort, then thought better of it. Instead he stared directly at Lucien, slowly unzipped his overalls and shrugged out of the top part to reveal his sweat-streaked chest. Then he picked up the handles of the wheelbarrow, smiled innocently and walked away. His intent was to show Lucien that he wasn't quite so pliable after all. He looked back over his shoulder and winced. Lucien's wry smile suggested that it was more than likely that his attitude would be rewarded with punishment. Ben's cock burned at the thought—perhaps he should practice a bit more belligerence.

For an autumn day it was unseasonably warm. Ben rested on a hay bale while Lucien fetched glasses of iced water from the house.

"Here, you've earned this." Lucien handed over a glass and Ben gulped the cold liquid down greedily. A few drops of water slid down his chin and he wiped them away. Lucien downed his drink in one long swallow. He put both glasses on the floor. "You work hard. I'm getting my money's worth so far."

Ben shoved some sweaty strands of hair away from his eyes. "If I wasn't here, would you be doing all this alone?"

"Horses don't clean out their own stables, unfortunately."

"Do you ever give a direct answer to a question?"

"Only when I choose to. Stand up." Lucien ran his tongue over his lower lip. Mesmerized, Ben watched the action as he stood. He took a couple of nervous steps back but there was a straw barrier behind him. The stalks scratched at his bare back. Lucien picked up a length of baling twine from the floor.

"Put out your hands."

Ben's glance traveled from the twine to Lucien's heated gaze. "I don't think…"

"Don't think. Obey. Or this concept too difficult for you?"

Shaking, Ben held his arms out in front of him.

"Put your wrists together."

"What are you going to do?"

Lucien raised an eyebrow and waited until Ben did as he'd been asked. He pressed his wrists together and closed his eyes.

"No. I want you to watch what I'm doing."

Ben blinked. Lucien wound the twine around Ben's wrists and tied it off with a bow. Ben's cock hardened and pressed against the rough canvas of the overalls. Lucien pulled him close with a hand on his arse. Their bodies rubbed together and Ben discovered that Lucien was just as aroused as he was.

"I knew you'd get off on being bound." Lucien squeezed Ben's buttock.

"I don't! I mean... You are so bloody full of yourself, Lucien." Without realizing what he was doing, Ben leaned into Lucien's hold, seeking reassurance.

"You're quite safe with me," Lucien whispered in his ear before taking the lobe between his teeth and pulling a little. "We should get on with our work. The day will be over before we know it." He walked away leaving Ben to pull with his teeth at the ties restraining him. They fell away easily enough, leaving shallow grooves on his skin. He rubbed at the marks, but stopped. For some strange reason he liked to see them there.

* * * *

The day passed quickly. Resetting some fence posts, digging a drainage ditch and trimming a couple of trees with dangerous branches followed mucking out. It had been hard, physical labor and by the time the sun had started to dip below the horizon, Ben was exhausted.

If anything, Lucien had worked even harder. They had both ended up topless and Ben had enjoyed watching the strength evident in Lucien's lean frame, but now they had stopped working the air felt chilly on his skin. He zipped up his overalls and followed Lucien back toward the house. They had eaten a packed lunch out in the field and had shared a flask of coffee, but his stomach was starting to complain.

He jumped as Lucien wrapped a strong arm around his shoulders. "Thank you for today. I couldn't have done any of those jobs on my own."

Ben didn't push him away. "Don't you have staff to do this stuff?"

"I wish! I *am* the staff when it comes to hard labor around this place. If I don't do it, it doesn't get done. James has a couple of laborers but they are all far too busy with the farm, and Maddy has the house and family to deal with. We can't afford to employ more people."

"But…you're a lord! The car, the house… Surely you don't need to work like this?"

"Don't believe everything you read about the aristocracy, Ben. The house is a money pit, the maintenance bills are never-ending—it's worse than painting the Forth Bridge. The car was my father's and it's my one indulgence. I take a good salary from the estate, but, believe me, I have to work for it. Can't do anything about the title, I'm afraid. You'll have to live with that."

Ben stayed quiet. The more he discovered about Lucien Thorne, the more he liked him. Of course, he was still obnoxiously arrogant and Ben constantly wavered between wanting to hit the man and kiss him. Lucien lowered his arm to circle his waist, and a tingling spread across Ben's skin.

He tried to distract himself with more questions. "I thought you had a law degree?"

"Been doing some research, have you?"

"No! And I certainly haven't been following you around for the last six months. People at the club talk about you all the time, you must know that."

"Okay! Point taken. Yes, you're right. I handle all the estate's legal work and do some pro bono stuff for local charities. I read law because my father wanted me to — it was never my career choice. It comes in handy and I enjoy the challenge, but I'd never be able to do it full-time."

"So what would you have studied if you'd been able to choose?"

"Classics. I love Greek and Roman history."

Another surprise. Ben was saved from responding as they reached the house and Lucien let him go. He immediately missed the feeling of a strong arm around him and sighed at his own vulnerability.

"Maddy promised to leave us something for dinner, but we'll take it back to my place. I'll give you the tour first, if you're interested?"

"Definitely!" Ben immediately forgot his rumbling belly. The house was really interesting, and he could just imagine it as the set for a period drama or even a gothic horror. It would make a great haunted house.

* * * *

Lucien proved to be a knowledgeable guide, pointing out all the little quirks in the architecture and decoration. The place was full of eclectic collections of different kinds, some great tapestries and two secret passages.

"It was something of a gothic fancy for the architect, and it's not quite as old as it looks — early Victorian, in fact."

That made a lot of sense, considering the contents. "So do you have any filming going on at the moment?" Ben admired a huge landscape painting, then turned to look at Lucien.

"One crew have just left. They were making a horror flick — seemed to be forever cleaning up fake blood spatter. The hire contracts always state that the house has to be left in the condition it was found and most production companies are really careful. A bad reputation would spread to other locations quickly enough. Another lot are due tomorrow and they'll be here for three months. Something Dickensian, I think." He shrugged. "I usually try to stay out of the way. Maddy handles that side of things. Anyway, enough talking. I'm starving."

They collected a hamper from the kitchen, locked up the house, then walked the quarter-mile path to the gamekeeper's house. It was tucked back out of sight in a small copse of trees, and it was very quiet.

"Wow, it's so peaceful here," Ben commented. "I can't hear any traffic noise at all."

"We're a good distance from the nearest road. It's a great spot for watching the night sky as well. There's very little light pollution out here and you'd be amazed what a difference it makes."

"You're a star gazer?" Ben absorbed yet another facet of his intriguing host.

"Nothing so grand. I just like to lie out here sometimes and watch the sky. You should have seen the Perseids meteor showers in August, they were spectacular."

"I can imagine." Ben thought how nice it would be to lie with Lucien under a summer sky gazing at the heavens.

"Come on, let's go inside."

Lucien pushed open the front door, which didn't appear to be locked. The hall was surprisingly modern. Ben had been expecting Victorian décor to match the building but the walls were painted in a fresh cream. Dark polished parquet covered the floor and the space smelled of polish.

"I'll unpack the food if you want the first shower?" Lucien said. "Bathroom's upstairs on the right."

Lucien didn't wait for an answer, but disappeared through a door that Ben assumed led to the kitchen. He climbed the stairs, painfully aware of his aching muscles, and pushed open the first door he came to. It wasn't a bathroom, but what he assumed was Lucien's bedroom. Curious, Ben flicked on the light. The room was decorated in a deep burgundy color, set off by small lights set into the ceiling rather than one central pendant. The varnished floorboards were covered with thick rugs and the two windows were draped with dark velvet. His gaze skirted over the oak furniture to the huge four-poster bed and its dark silk canopy. He found himself blushing as thoughts of what could happen there flashed across his mind. Hurriedly, he flicked the lights off and went to find the bathroom instead.

The next door Ben tried was the correct one.

"Wow, it's huge!" He took in a massive roll-top tub, separate walk-in shower and sleek modern sink and toilet. Half the room was tiled, the other painted in a restful shade of duck-egg blue. Granite tiles covered the floor, the deep gray softened by mats that matched the paint.

Half of Ben's bedsit would fit in the luxurious space. He fiddled with the knobs in the shower cubicle and soon warmed the room with steaming spray. He stripped off his filthy overalls and underwear, piling them in a heap in one corner. It crossed his mind that his clothes were still in the boot room at the main house. Lucien wasn't that much taller than him — he could borrow some old clothes no doubt.

Ben stepped beneath the spray and gave a happy sigh. Compared to his own temperamental shower, this was sheer heaven. Lucien's shower gel smelled of freshly mown grass. Deciding that there had to be some pay off for twenty-four hours of indentured servitude, Ben helped himself to a huge dollop and set about getting clean.

* * * *

Lucien laid the kitchen table and spread out the food that his sister had prepared — cooked meats, cheese and pâté with homemade bread formed the main course, with a range of salad accompaniments. For dessert there were miniature fruit tartlets. He admired the pricey bottle of merlot and extracted the cork to allow the wine to breathe. Maddy had done a good job, bless her. It was just what they needed after a hard day's work. If he'd been alone, he might have managed a cheese and pickle sandwich. This was a great improvement.

He smiled to himself. The whole day had been a step up from his usual, monotonous routine. Watching Ben work up a sweat had been so tempting. All that lean muscle flexing beneath smooth, golden skin. He'd had to resist the urge to take the boy there and then, out in the fields — to pin him down in the grass and claim what was his. He was quite impressed by his own willpower.

"Patience, Lucien," he murmured. "One step at a time." A slow hunt would be all the more pleasurable when he finally took his prey. It was easy to think of Ben in those terms. Half the time he resembled a startled fawn. But there were also the intriguing hints of a more spirited nature behind the fragile shell, and Lucien relished the challenge of a little resistance. He waited until he heard the shower start to run, selected a riding crop from a hook next to the door then followed Ben upstairs. Excitement made Lucien's heart beat a little quicker. The bathroom door was open a crack but the room was nicely steamed, allowing him to slip inside and wait without being seen. Ben was humming softly to himself and Lucien could see the outline of his body through the opaque glass of the shower screen.

Ben really was delicious. Lucien pictured him bound and helpless on his knees, water cascading from his back and shoulders as he parted his lips and took Lucien into his mouth, tiny glittering droplets decorating his lashes. Lucien licked his lips and allowed himself to imagine what it would be like to press Ben against the tiles. He would resist, of course — that was part of the fun. But eventually he would melt against Lucien's body and open to him. Lucien had to suppress a moan. His cock ached and his balls felt tight and heavy. If Ben didn't get out of the shower soon, Lucien thought he might have to go in and drag him out. In the meantime, he had to satisfy himself with observing the misty curves of Ben's body and his fluid movements.

Ben sluiced shampoo through his hair and massaged gel into his tired limbs. He sighed happily. Despite a somewhat stressful start, it had been a good day and he had caught a few brief glimpses of a softer side of Lucien — albeit tempered by a healthy dose of grouch. If there was a walking definition of an alpha male, Lucien was it. He carried it off well. Everything about him — from the way he walked and held himself to his tone of voice and narrowed glare — exuded command. Ben's cock twitched at the thought and he squeezed his eyes shut, trying to exert some control over his body.

He turned the shower to cold for a refreshing final blast and sucked in a sharp breath as the spray hit him before quickly turning it off. He pushed open the cubicle door and froze.

Lucien's smile would have suited a wolf staring down an injured rabbit. He stood with his legs braced, slapping the leather strap at the end of a riding crop into the open palm of his hand. Ben cringed as leather hit skin but his cock jerked. He tried to reach for a towel, only to be intercepted.

"No. I don't think so."

Lucien ran his tongue across his lower lip and Ben waited for him to make the next move. He knew his expression must be priceless — this moment would stay with him for the rest of his life. Shock, fear and desire fought for dominance. Ben tried to cover his half-hard dick with his hands, only to have them pushed away by the end of the crop.

"Behind your back. Now."

"Lucien... Please..." Confusion and mild panic overwhelmed him.

The low growl at the back of Lucien's throat announced his displeasure, and Ben hurriedly took a step back whilst doing as he had been told. He felt so vulnerable and exposed, his dick swelling and rising, totally out of his control.

Lucien lifted the hardening member with the end of the short whip and curled his lip into a contemptuous sneer.

"I hope you weren't trying to hide this from me, Benedict. I'm pleased that you shaved yourself, but I'm afraid you still have to be punished."

Under Lucien's guidance, the crop began to journey gently down his thigh, then up across his taut stomach muscles. Ben hardly dared to breathe.

"What did I do? You can't..."

His voice broke as Lucien flicked one of his aching nipples, then the other.

"Your little stunt with the wheelbarrow this morning didn't go unnoticed. Did you think I would let you get away with such a lack of respect?"

Lucien moved closer, a predator stalking his prey, trailing leather lightly across skin still beaded with water from the shower.

Ben shivered, though he was anything but cold. He was achingly hard and his balls felt like hot coals between his legs.

"I'm sorry, Lucien. I didn't mean—"

"Quiet. I didn't give you permission to speak. And I think you knew exactly what you were doing. Taunting me with your body."

He tapped Ben's inner thighs, forcing him to stand with his legs farther apart.

"Bend over and hold the edge of the bath."

Ben suppressed his rising panic and took a small step toward the huge roll-top tub, but didn't bend down.

"I can't do this."

Lucien hissed his impatience. "Disobey me and I'll just punish you more, Benedict." He applied some weight to Ben's resistant shoulder and Ben gave way, bending to grasp the edge of the bath with shaking hands.

"Better." Lucien ran his weapon over one tense cheek, then dragged the leather across the back of Ben's hanging balls. Ben's arse muscles clenched as his sensitive flesh was grazed over and over again, and he could almost feel Lucien's satisfied smile behind him. He turned to see what his tormentor was up to.

Without warning, Lucien drew back his arm and slashed the crop across Ben's arse. The resulting gasp was part pain, part indignation and part pleasure. He did it again, then a third time before standing back.

Ben choked back a sob. His backside was on fire but the threat of orgasm was only a touch away, something that Lucien didn't grant.

"I've left you some clothes on my bed. Get dry, get dressed and get downstairs." Lucien went to the door. "If your hands go anywhere near your cock for any purpose other than to get dry, I will know. No getting excited without my permission. Do you understand?"

Ben nodded.

"Out loud, please."

"Yes, Lucien. I understand."

As soon as the door had closed, Ben sank to the floor and wrapped his arms around his knees. He squirmed as his sore flesh made contact with the damp bath mat. What the hell had he done? He should have refused to submit. Now Lucien would assume that he could do whatever the hell he wanted. Ben resisted the urge to fondle his aching and still-hard dick. How could his body and his mind have two such different opinions on his treatment?

He shivered and realized that he was starting to get cold. He struggled shakily to his feet and rubbed himself down with a soft towel, wincing as the fabric made contact with his tender arse. How many times was he going to be reminded of what Lucien had done? He could just about see the red stripes in the mirror. Lucien hadn't hit him hard enough to cause any real damage. It had hurt, but every stroke had sent a jolt of pleasure to his groin and he hadn't wanted it to end. That was something that he definitely wouldn't be admitting to. He took his time getting dressed. Making Lucien wait was one small act of rebellion he could manage.

Chapter Nine

Lucien had clearly found somewhere else to shower by the time Ben had plucked up the courage to go downstairs and face him. He looked fresh and annoyingly relaxed. He made no comment about how long it had taken Ben to join him.

"Sit down. You must be hungry." Lucien smiled gently. "You're going to need your strength."

Ben gave him a worried look but didn't rise to the bait. Lucien knew exactly how to keep him off balance. He sat carefully, ignoring the knowing gleam in Lucien's blue eyes. Lucien pushed a loaded plate toward him.

"Eat. Maddy has done us proud."

When Ben took the first bite of fresh bread he realized just how ravenous he was. The food was good, and for a while he could ignore his doubts, let his taste buds dance and enjoy the mellow warmth of fine red wine.

Lucien's eyes never left him. The palpable tension in the air built slowly but steadily until Ben could bear it no longer.

"I know I shouldn't ask, but what exactly are your plans for the rest of the evening?"

"You're right. You shouldn't ask."

"You're scaring me, Lucien."

Lucien pushed a plate of sweet tartlets toward him, but Ben's appetite had dissipated.

"I have you for another twelve hours yet, and all you have to do is listen and obey. That's what you agree to."

Ben shivered. "I know, but..." He ran out of words. He couldn't think straight. He should make some kind of decision, but it was too difficult. Lucien would decide. Ben just had to stop worrying and give up any pretense at controlling the situation.

Lucien stood and walked around the table. He stood behind him and caressed the back of Ben's neck with one hand, massaging the tense muscles. "If you've had enough to eat, let's go upstairs and I'll show you, instead."

He took him by the wrist—not the hand—and guided him toward the stairs. Everything the man did seemed to have an element of control. His touch was light but firm. Ben knew instinctively that if he tried to pull away, the grip would just tighten, so he remained pliant and allowed Lucien to lead him.

Once they were inside the bedroom, Lucien shut the door firmly behind them. He lit two fat, white candles that sat on a shelf and pulled the heavy drapes. The lighting was subtle and illumination flickered across the walls. Ben caught the scents of vanilla and spice and tried to relax. His own reflection in the dresser mirror told him that he wasn't doing a very good job of it. Anxiety showed clearly in his gray eyes, and his hair stuck up in spikes where he'd rubbed his hands agitatedly through it.

"Are you okay?" Lucien pushed one silky strand of hair away from Ben's face.

"Why? Would it make any difference if I wasn't?"

The words were abrupt and Ben hung his head, afraid of Lucien's reaction.

"You can leave any time you want to, Ben. You have absolutely no reason to be afraid. I'm not going to force you to do anything you don't want to, promise or not. There is a spare bedroom along the hall which is yours to use if you wish."

Lucien's tone was soft and gentle—he didn't betray any hint of the frustration he might be feeling.

Ben looked longingly at the door, but made no attempt to move toward it. Out there was safety—the easy path—but that wasn't what he wanted. The promise was irrelevant. Ben needed to discover where Lucien could take him. He reached out with one hand to touch Lucien's gleaming, black hair.

It seemed to be all the confirmation Lucien needed. One step back re-established who was in control.

"I want you to strip to the waist."

Ben hesitated for just a few seconds before slowly undoing his buttons of his borrowed shirt and pulling the shirt-tails from his waistband. He shrugged the fabric from his shoulders and let it drop to the floor. He held his head up, maintaining eye contact until Lucien walked around him, as if examining every inch of Ben's smooth skin. Ben heard a drawer slide open and when Lucien returned to face him, he was holding something in his hands.

"Hold out your arm." Lucien buckled a heavy, black leather cuff around Ben's slim wrist, pulling the strap tight. He repeated the process with the other wrist and Ben felt the inevitable burn of excitement at his groin. Each cuff had a small metal loop attached to the inside, and Ben was nervously curious as to how they might be used.

"Not too tight?"

Lucien's question gave Ben some reassurance that he would be handled with care.

"No. They're fine."

"Sir." Lucien waited expectantly.

"They're fine, Sir." Ben's voice cracked a little.

Lucien gestured with his head to the front bedpost. Ben turned and looked up. In the semi-darkness, they were hard to see, but near the top of the posts were two small hooks screwed into the wood. He swallowed, visualizing the D-rings on his cuffs.

"Those hooks have nothing to do with curtains." Lucien's smile was pure evil. "Take off your shoes and socks and stand with your back to the bed."

The fine hairs on the backs of Ben's arms stood on end. He found it hard to catch his breath and gave himself a mental cheer when he managed to remove his footwear without falling on his arse. He backed up to the foot of the bed and waited for Lucien to instruct him further.

Once Ben was in a satisfactory position, Lucien lifted one arm, then the other, slipping the cuff rings over the small hooks until Ben's arms were pulled high and wide. He stood back as if to admire his victim, watching as Ben tested the strength of the rings. With both arms restrained, he couldn't reach high enough to get himself free, and there was absolutely no give from the solid posts. He was stuck until Lucien decided to let him go.

He hoped that Lucien was finding it as hard to control his feelings as he was. He had not dreamed that Lucien would push him this far. His muscles strained. His erection was painful and Lucien's arousal was evident under the stressed material of his trousers. Ben couldn't wait to see the delights beneath, even if he had to suffer for the sight.

"I was going to blindfold you—you looked so wonderful waiting for me this morning—but I've reconsidered and decided that I would rather you see what's coming. I want you to anticipate every touch. Everything I do to you, I'm going to describe before it happens." Lucien leaned in and whispered into Ben's ear, "You will not come. Understand? Not until I say you can."

"But what if I can't help myself, Sir?" Ben whispered.

"Then you'll be punished." Lucien's tone was so matter of fact, he could have been discussing the weather.

"I don't think…"

"Hush." Lucien pressed a finger to Ben's lips. "Stop worrying."

Ben drew the tip of Lucien's finger into his mouth and sucked. Lucien smiled indulgently before gently drawing away. He stripped off his shirt, and Ben couldn't help but stare. Lucien was stunning. Ben imagined licking each of the rippling abs. It wasn't going to take much to bring him to the brink. He was close enough already—whether he could do as Lucien had commanded and keep control of his body was debatable. Still, if he did come without permission Lucien would have another excuse to punish him and, as much as he hated to admit it, that was a win-win situation. Not that Lucien would need an excuse.

"Give me your safeword. Use it and I stop. Immediately."

Ben's heart was pounding. What the hell was Lucien planning that required a safeword?

"You do know what a safeword is?"

Ben nodded. "I'm not totally naïve."

That brought a smile to Lucien's lips. "No, you're not, are you?"

Oh God. "River." It was the first word that came into Ben's mind.

"Okay. Remember, that word leaves your lips and this stops. Immediately. We'll talk before anything else happens. It's my job to recognize your limits, Ben, but if you get scared — if I do anything you don't like — use that word."

Ben bit down on his lower lip in the hope that pain would provide a distraction and prayed that Lucien wouldn't touch him. He could feel the pre-cum slicking the tip of his engorged dick and he thought his balls might catch fire they were so hot and tight. Just the anticipation of what Lucien might have planned was torture, and being bound was turning him on in a way he never would have thought possible.

He focused his eyes and whimpered at the sight of what Lucien held in his hand. The slim metal stick had a small, spiked wheel on the end, which Lucien casually rotated with one finger.

"So, you know what this is, then?"

"It's a pinwheel. I've seen them on the Internet."

"Have you been investigating kinky websites, Ben?"

"Maybe." Ben ducked his head.

"I think you'll find that experience, in the flesh as it were, proves to be a hundred times more satisfying." Lucien put far too much emphasis on the word 'satisfying'. "This little tool is going to help me discover which parts of your delicious body are the most sensitive to pain."

Ben knew that there would only be a tiny difference in pressure between bearable pain and broken skin. The spikes were very sharp. He watched as Lucien tested it on the inside of his arm and relaxed—he trusted Lucien not to hurt him too much.

"I'm going to run this across your skin, starting with less...delicate areas." Lucien ran the wheel across Ben's abdomen, leaving behind tracks of red dots. There was no blood, just a trail of indentations. Ben whimpered and fought his restraints as the wheel tracked from beneath one arm, down his rib, then around his lower back. The sting sent lightning strikes of arousal directly to his cock.

Lucien stroked the marks he'd created and looked thoughtful. "I wonder how my little friend will feel here?" He flicked Ben's hardened nipple and smirked as Ben tried to jerk away from him.

Lucien put the pinwheel down on the bed and tackled Ben's waistband instead.

"I think I need a better view first and considerably more access."

He yanked Ben's trousers down and pushed them away, exposing tight black shorts, steeply tented and already damp.

"It seems you are enjoying this a little too much."

Lucien's fingers hovered directly over the bulge of Ben's cloth-covered erection. One touch and Ben wouldn't be able to hold back the orgasm that threatened to consume him. He sobbed.

"Oh yes, far too much pleasure. I need to be less lenient with you."

Ben moaned his disagreement as Lucien applied the torturously sharp wheel to his inner thigh.

Fuck, it hurt. He didn't dare to think what it might feel like on more sensitive flesh. He wished Lucien would take some more of his clothes off. Maybe if they were both naked he might feel slightly less vulnerable—probably not, but at the very least it would give him something else to take his mind off his aching wrists, throbbing cock and stinging skin.

"I don't want to give you the impression that I'm feeling any pity, but I'm in a generous mood, so I'm going to give you a choice now." Lucien smiled sweetly and Ben just knew that he wasn't going to like his options.

Lucien flicked his warm tongue across Ben's throbbing nipples, and Ben couldn't stop the gasp of pleasure that escaped his lips.

"Clamps or the wheel here?"

"Fuck!" *That tongue again.*

"That's not an appropriate answer, Benedict." Lucien began to place deceptively gentle kisses along Ben's shoulder.

"It's hardly a fair choice!"

"I don't do fair. Choose."

"All right! Clamps." *No way I want those spikes digging into my nipples.*

As soon as Ben saw the satisfied grin on Lucien's face, he realized that he'd made a huge mistake.

"Oh, fuck. You wouldn't."

"You know I would. The choice applied to these." Lucien pinched both nipples hard. "I didn't mention other parts of your body."

He wandered across to the dresser and rummaged in a drawer.

"Hmm. So many choices. Yes! These are perfect."

He returned to face Ben, swinging a short chain, letting it wrap around his fingers.

"These are rubber-tipped clamps, they're spring-loaded and quite painful. Not as bad as alligator clips, though, these won't bite into your flesh. I'll save those for another time."

Ben's nipples had already hardened into aching nubs but Lucien flicked them a couple of times anyway. He squeezed open the clamp.

"Have you worn these before?"

Ben shook his head.

"Untouched. So perfect." Lucien leaned in and kissed him. "This will ache. The burn will build gradually but the real fire won't start until I take them off." He attached one clamp, which was linked by a slender chain to its twin. He applied the second quickly and efficiently, then stepped back.

"They look good on you." He tugged on the chain.

Ben squirmed as he tried to get used to the inescapable sensation that threatened to push him over the edge. Only the thought of what Lucien might do if he came without permission kept him teetering on the brink of orgasm. His nipples had always been sensitive but he hadn't realized how every tug connected directly to his balls.

"I should clamp you while we row. Just think how that tight shirt I gave you will rub against them with every stroke." Lucien jiggled the chain again. "What do you think?"

"I think you're a sadistic bastard. Sir."

"An accurate assessment." Lucien picked up the pinwheel from its resting place on the bed. "I should live up to the reputation, shouldn't I?"

Through the clingy cotton of Ben's increasingly damp underwear, the pinwheel wasn't too bad, but that relief wasn't going to last.

Lucien stood back and watched as Ben tried not to hyperventilate.

"It was very accommodating of you to make a choice that allowed me to use the wheel on your cock. I think it's time to take a proper look, don't you?"

"Bastard!" Ben fought his restraints desperately, but it was no use. The cool metal of sharp scissors grazed his hip as Lucien sliced neatly through the side seams of his underwear and pulled the offending garment away.

"That's much better." Lucien sounded like the cat who'd got the cream, the smoked salmon and the roast chicken all in one go.

He ran the pinwheel along the length of Ben's rigid cock with no warning. Ben yelled and came instantly. The increased level of pain and pleasure had been just too much to cope with.

Lucien laughed in delight. "You have no idea how much trouble you are in now."

His face burning, Ben looked at him with all the defiance he could muster. "Do your worst. I won't break my word."

Lucien gave him a pitying look. "You'll see nowhere near my worst tonight, I can assure you. However, I did plan a little treat for you."

He went back to his toy drawer and pulled out something made of clear plastic. Ben couldn't see what it was, but the look on Lucien's face suggested that he wasn't going to like it.

"It's good that you lost control, Benedict. It means I can discipline you more, which—as I think you've probably worked out by now—I really enjoy. It also means I can use my new toy on you. It won't go on when you're hard."

Ben tensed as he realized what it was that Lucien was holding.

"You can't put that on me!"

"How do you intend to stop me?" Lucien gave a deep chuckle. "The look on your face is just perfect. This" — he held up the complicated piece of acrylic — "is a chastity device, something I think would be good for you to get used to, but I digress. This one is a little different—it's lined with flexible spikes. As soon as you get hard, they'll dig in, which I imagine is going to cause you not insignificant discomfort." He snapped the device in place and stood back to admire his handiwork.

Ben could feel the spikes already, and the weight of the device. He spread his legs a little farther, trying to reduce the pressure, but there was no escape from the sensation. It was maddening not to be able to get any relief, and he yanked on his restraints in frustration.

"It looks amazing. Let's see if it works."

Lucien reached between Ben's legs and stroked his balls with the tip of one finger.

"Son of a bitch!" Ben squirmed away from his touch and received a sharp slap to his arse.

"Keep still."

Lucien narrowed his eyes and Ben's heart leaped. That look did things to him that ought to be against the law. The heat in his groin was already building.

Think pure thoughts. Think pure thoughts. He repeated the mantra over and over in his head, squeezing his eyes shut, flinching inwardly at the touch he knew would come. When it didn't, he tentatively opened his eyes to see Lucien taking his trousers off.

"Oh, fuck!" The sight of him clad only in hip-skimming briefs did what the touch had not quite managed, and Ben's cock swelled into aching rigidity. The flexible points in the sleeve of the chastity device pressed hard into all the most sensitive parts of his flesh, and the moan that escaped him was pure frustration.

"A little denial will be good for you, Benedict." Lucien stroked himself through the fabric of his underwear and produced his most evil smirk as Ben forced himself to take short, rapid breaths.

"I'm going to explore you now. I want to discover every erogenous zone you possess."

He let his hands start wandering across Ben's body, touching and stroking. He flicked the nipple clamps when they came into range and ran his nail across the sensitive skin surrounding them.

"Jesus Christ!" Ben was in agony and ecstasy. He had never experienced such an explosive feeling of pleasure.

Lucien moved behind him and sat on the end of the bed, straddling Ben. The soft skin of Lucien's thighs rubbed against him, then his vision blurred as Lucien stroked and squeezed his arse, rubbing between his cheeks and circling the tight bud of his entrance. When Lucien replaced fingers with his tongue, Ben screamed. His cock burned. The agony of not being able to release was all-consuming. He shook in his bonds and whimpered pitifully.

"Stop! Please, stop!"

Of course, that was exactly the motivation Lucien needed to continue and Ben had not used the safeword. Lucien probed a little deeper with his tongue and, at the same time, he grabbed Ben's balls and squeezed.

"Holy fuck!" Ben sobbed, tears streaming down his face. It was too much. "River! Please, Lucien!"

Lucien stopped what he was doing instantly. Ben barely noticed as his body jerked and shook. When his arms were lowered, he didn't register that he was free. Lucien laid him back on the bed and kissed away the tears.

"Hush, baby. It's all right. Relax."

Ben shuddered and gradually calmed until he could focus on Lucien's soft blue eyes.

"You stopped."

"Of course I did. You used your safeword."

"It was too much."

"Too much pain?" Lucien asked, stroking Ben's hair.

"Too much pleasure," he admitted. "Now let me out of this contraption." He tapped the hard plastic sheath around his cock.

"No."

Lucien stretched out on the bed next to him.

"What do you mean, no? Take it off!"

"Ben, your promise lasts until eight tomorrow morning. You are going to sleep in this bed next to me. You are going to keep the wrist cuffs on and this"—he stroked the chastity device—"stays. You didn't safeword when I put it on you."

Ben bashed his head back against the pillow, and Lucien laughed. "You should also know that it's not locked."

"Unbelievable!" Ben drew his knees up. "You're not doing anything to convince me that a relationship with you would be a good idea."

Lucien slipped off his underwear and began to fondle his rigid shaft. "I don't need to convince you of anything. If you hadn't already made up your mind, there's no way you would have put up with the way I've treated you today." He moved his hand faster.

Ben scowled. Lucien was infuriatingly close to the truth.

"So why haven't you...?"

"Fucked you?"

Suddenly shy, Ben nodded.

Lucien's hand blurred as he rubbed himself faster and faster until he shot all over his thigh with a sigh of satisfaction.

"Willing or not, Ben, you're here because I paid a lot of money to make sure you were. I won't take your virginity while there's even the remotest chance that you might feel obligated."

"My... How the hell did you know?"

Lucien leaned over and kissed him deeply. "I was ninety-nine percent sure, but you've just confirmed it."

Ben was exhausted. He ached everywhere, his dick throbbed uncomfortably in its restrictive case, his wrists were sore, but he felt deeply content. Lucien had just confirmed what he had known deep down—that he might be an evil bastard, but he could also be thoughtful, caring and considerate.

"I knew there was a soft center beneath that satanic exterior."

Lucien plucked both clamps from Ben's nipples at the same time. Ben screamed as the tender flesh awakened and fire burned his chest. Lucien tossed the clamps aside and began to manipulate Ben's tortured flesh.

Tears rolled from Ben's eyes. The pain was sweetly intense. He craved Lucien's touch yet wanted to push him away. The agony faded to a dull throb and Lucien got up.

"Don't go." Ben hated how needy he sounded.

"I'm just going to fetch something to clean us up. I won't be a minute." He disappeared, before returning with a damp towel, which he used to gently wipe the stickiness from Ben's skin before tending to himself.

He tossed the cloth aside, then climbed into bed and pulled the covers over the two of them.

"Soft center. Definitely." Ben wriggled a little closer to Lucien's warmth.

"We'll see if you think the same when the alarm goes off at eight tomorrow morning."

Suddenly, all Ben's nerves returned. "Why? What do you mean?"

He jerked as Lucien slid a hand toward his groin, then tapped the plastic encasing Ben's cock.

"Go to sleep, Ben, or I might just find the padlock for this thing and then lose the key."

Ben squeezed his eyes shut and resisted the urge to grab a pillow and beat Lucien with it. It was going to be a long night.

Chapter Ten

Ben woke long before the alarm went off. It wasn't the first time either. Dreams of Lucien had excited his dormant cock, and spiky punishment had automatically been administered several times throughout the slow hours of darkness. He desperately needed to come. The constant cycle of arousal, pain and frustration had turned him into a bundle of nerves, but stubborn pride would not allow him to remove the chastity device before his promise had been fulfilled.

He wished he could have enjoyed the comfort of the beautiful four-poster more. The expensive sheets were cool and smooth. The duvet was cloud-light but warm, enclosed in a black silk cover that matched Lucien's hair.

Ben turned to look at the man sleeping next to him. Thick, dark lashes fluttered against pale cheeks. Lush lips were slightly parted, and Ben felt an irresistible urge to kiss them. He leaned over and brushed Lucien's mouth with his own, pulling back hesitantly as the steady rise and fall rhythm of Lucien's chest altered slightly.

"You really are a glutton for punishment, aren't you?" Lucien's eyes didn't open but a cruel smile played across his lips, which had seemed so tempting just a few seconds earlier. "What time is it?"

"Just after seven." Ben was already regretting the impetuous kiss.

Lucien stretched languorously. "Almost an hour left, then. Plenty of time to torment you." He propped himself up on his pillows. "Come and kneel across my lap."

Ben swallowed. "Why?"

"Don't question me, Benedict. Do as I say." Lucien's tone lashed the air like a whip.

Slowly Ben complied, parting his legs wide to straddle Lucien's thighs. The bed covers pooled around Ben's hips and he shivered as the cool air caressed his chest and groin. He flushed at the thought of what he must look like. His gaze drifted down to drink in the sight of Lucien's magnificent erection and the neatly cropped hair that bedded its root.

Ben's cock throbbed painfully in its cruel prison. Lucien reached beneath the device and stroked Ben's balls. Ben's muscles tensed as Lucien's touch caused his tortured cock to swell even further. Lucien moved his hands to circle Ben's slim waist, brushing the flat plane of his stomach with both thumbs. Ben flinched and gripped the covers with both hands.

"You are so beautiful, Ben. I could look at you for hours."

Ben's cheeks burned. He felt defenseless, displayed like this. He desperately wanted the sensation of Lucien's silky skin beneath his fingers, but hardly dared to ask. He took a deep breath.

"May I touch you?"

Lucien blinked. "If I allow that, what do I get in return?" Lucien slid his hands around to Ben's back and stroked the curve of his arse.

Ben lowered his eyes. "What do you want?"

"You know what I want, Ben. You."

Ben sighed and met Lucien's eyes. "You already have me. You know that." It was the truth. Ben could no more escape Lucien's thrall than pull away from his touch.

"I just needed to hear you say it."

Gently, Ben wrapped his hand around the satiny skin of Lucien's cock. It was warm and alive to his touch, twitching with need. He squeezed lightly, familiarizing himself with the solid girth of it before brushing the pad of his thumb across the shiny, moist tip. He slid his hand down and tentatively cupped the weight of Lucien's sac, before massaging it tenderly.

He was so focused on what he was doing that he didn't notice the anguished look on Lucien's face until a hiss escaped his lips. "Fuck, Ben, if this is your idea of vengeance, it's working."

Ben chuckled. "Sorry, I didn't think. But revenge is a good idea."

He flicked his fingers gently before taking a firm grasp of Lucien's cock once more. "Perhaps I could persuade you to release me?"

"No. Not before eight."

Ben began to squeeze and release his grip rhythmically, but as soon as Lucien's muscles tensed as if he was about to come, Ben let go.

"Denial is good for you—I think that's what you said?" Ben gazed innocently down into a thunderous expression.

"Denying me will not be good for *you*, Ben, I can assure you. How would you like to have your cock locked up for the rest of your life? It's going to happen if you don't finish what you started."

Ben was tempted to laugh, but then caught the gleam in Lucien's eyes. *Fuck, he actually means it.* Ben applied his hand again with renewed vigor, and was rewarded with a gasp and a hand covered with warm cream.

He let Lucien recover for a few moments before asking, "Am I allowed to go to the bathroom?"

"Of course. But don't come back without coffee. I can be especially unpleasant without my morning hit."

Ben shook his head in exasperation. "Fine. How do you like it?"

"Black."

Ben clambered out of bed, trying not to move awkwardly with the heavy plastic casing around his dick. He made use of some tissues to clean his hand, then went to grab his trousers.

"No, no. What do you think you're doing?" Lucien scolded. "You go naked."

"You're kidding me?" Ben stared at him, hands on hips.

"It is not in me to kid you. Just be careful with the hot water."

Ben clenched his jaw but did as he had been told, deliberately wiggling his arse as he left the room. He could feel Lucien's smirk and gaze drilling into his back. Just the thought of him looking was enough to make Ben's cock twitch, and that didn't help his state of mind in the least.

He padded downstairs to the kitchen and leaned against the counter waiting for the kettle to boil. Lucien had ground coffee and a cafetière rather than a machine, so he spooned grounds into the jug, added water then gave it a stir before depressing the plunger. He rinsed the mugs they had used the previous evening rather than searching through cupboards for new ones and filled them. He climbed the stairs slowly, keeping the hot drinks level. He was horribly aware of his own nudity. His cheeks flushed at the thought of Lucien seeing the front view of his body. The plastic casing holding his cock pushed it away from his groin but compressed his balls slightly.

As Ben entered the bedroom, Lucien licked his lips and was clearly reveling in the power he had over Ben's body. His eyes were firmly fixed on Ben's groin.

"Your coffee, Sir." Ben couldn't help the hint of sarcasm in his tone. He placed one mug on the cabinet next to Lucien then took the other to his own side of the bed.

Ben knew he could have taken the chastity device off at any time during the night, but he hadn't. He'd been obedient even under extreme duress—he just didn't understand why. He was totally under Lucien's sway. That felt dangerous but very, very good. He slipped beneath the covers and took a couple of sips of his drink.

Two minutes later, the alarm went off and Ben heaved a shaky sigh of relief. He put his coffee down and leaned back against the pillows, about to do the hardest thing he'd ever done.

Lucien looked at him strangely. "Why aren't you taking it off? It has to be two minutes past by now. I thought you'd be desperate to be rid of it."

Ben took a deep breath and a leap into the unknown, his voice little more than a whisper. "I'm yours, Lucien. Sir. You should be the one to remove it."

"And what if I want it to stay?"

Ben sucked in a breath but steeled himself. "It's your decision. I'll do as you say."

Lucien yanked the covers back to expose Ben's lap. Gently, he triggered the release mechanism on the chastity device and slid the sheath carefully off. The inner spikes had left small red marks but had caused no worse damage.

"Ohhh! Thank God!" Ben shuddered with relief and squirmed beneath Lucien's careful touch. The light stroking of cool fingers was having an inevitable effect. Lucien kept his hand moving as he leaned across and kissed Ben hard. Ben responded with a heat and passion that came from somewhere deep inside. He grabbed strands of Lucien's dark hair and pulled him closer. Their mouths crushed together, tongues fighting for dominance. Lucien stroked Ben's cock harder and, painful though it was, Ben didn't want him to stop. His hips jerked as he pushed into Lucien's grip.

After twenty-four hours of frustration, when Ben came it was explosive. He threw his head back and screamed silently as the tension of the last day left him, along with ropes of cum that splattered his thighs. Sated and exhausted, Ben collapsed on to the mattress and Lucien stroked soft strands of hair away from his eyes.

"Feeling better?" The amused twist of his lips spoke volumes. "Christ, Ben, now I know what a little denial does to you…"

"No! Please, Lucien, not again…" Ben begged shamelessly, tears spiking in his eyes.

"Shh. It's all right. I'm not that cruel."

Ben raised one eyebrow and Lucien had the grace to look a little bashful.

"Okay. Well, maybe I am. But not now — not today. Still, I know what will make an effective punishment for you in future. I have a great belt that can keep your pretty cock locked away and your arse plugged."

"You wouldn't!" Ben's arse muscles clenched. "Of course you would, what am I saying?"

Lucien winked at him. He drained his mug and swung his long legs out of bed. "I hope you've got some energy left for rowing. We're late today, so we should avoid meeting Seb, which is always a bonus. I'll use the en suite, you can have the bathroom. If we shower together, neither of us will be in any condition to row anywhere."

"Okay." Ben tried not to be too obvious as he drooled over Lucien's body. "I'm curious, though. Did Seb know…about the promise?"

Lucien shook his head. "Not officially, no, but it doesn't take a genius to work it out. My family have made an annual five thousand pound gift to the club for over twenty years — that's too coincidental for even Seb's tiny brain to ignore."

He crossed the room with long, confident strides to the concealed door that hid the en-suite shower. "Besides, it's going to be pretty obvious from now on that we are together."

"Is it?" Ben perched on the side of the bed and looked back over his shoulder, trying to focus on Lucien's words rather than his arse.

"Definitely." Lucien didn't elucidate any further and disappeared into the shower. "And stop ogling my arse!" his voice echoed from behind the closed door.

Chapter Eleven

Dressed in rowing gear with track suits over the top, Ben and Lucien walked up to the main house to get Lucien's car. Ben wore another borrowed outfit, this time all black to match Lucien's. They took a detour to the house so that Ben could collect his clothes and small overnight bag from the boot room, then they returned the empty picnic hamper to the kitchen.

"Where is everyone?" Ben asked. "The house seems to be deserted."

"It is suspiciously quiet." Lucien frowned. "Normally this place is a war zone, though we aren't that early — the twins will be at school and that cuts the decibel level significantly." He shrugged. "With any luck we can make a clean getaway and avoid an interrogation from Maddy."

When they reached the stable yard, it became clear why the house had been empty. There was a confusing bustle of activity with cars and trucks scattered everywhere, horses being led out to grass, dogs barking and tons of electronic equipment lying in piles of boxes and crates.

Lucien's Aston was neatly boxed into a corner and he swore with some imagination. "Every fucking time. Film crews arrive and this place turns into fucking bedlam."

Ben gazed around, wide-eyed. "I think it's exciting."

"If you use that word again, little brother, I might have to wash your mouth out."

Ben couldn't stop the grin that spread across his face as Maddy reached up to hug Lucien.

"Good morning, Ben. I hope you didn't have to work too hard yesterday?" To his surprise, he got a hug too.

"No, I actually enjoyed myself, thanks. Oh, and the food you left was delicious."

"He fed you, then?" She smiled knowingly at Lucien. "And there was me thinking he had other things in mind for last night."

"Maddy!" Lucien protested, a hint of pink appearing on his cheeks.

"He must really like you, Ben. He's not denying it, did you notice that?"

Ben's face heated too as a cinematic version of the things he and Lucien had got up to the previous night was screened in his head. Lucien grabbed his arm and tugged.

"Benedict, get in the car and stop encouraging her. Maddy, get this fucking truck moved before I do something we'll all regret."

Ben put his bag into the Aston's boot and got into the passenger seat. The door closed with a satisfying clunk. Lucien slid gracefully into the driver's seat and shut his door.

"Let's get out of here. I need to work my frustrations out on the water." He turned the ignition on and lowered his window.

Maddy bent down to look in the car window. "Ben, you'd be very welcome to come and watch the filming if you are interested? The crew are setting up for pre-production today—the latest version of Great Expectations. Filming begins in a couple of days."

"I'd love to, if I wouldn't be in the way."

"Not at all. There will be plenty of odd jobs you can help with. I'll give Lucien all the details. I'm sure you'll be seeing a lot of him." She grinned. "And let me know if he gets too obnoxious—I'll up his babysitting duties."

By this point, Lucien was revving the car engine like a stallion pawing the ground. As soon as the lorry behind him edged away, tires spat gravel into the air and the powerful car leaped away, leaving Maddy laughing in the distance.

"Don't you dare say a word."

Ben wisely kept quiet, turning his head to try to hide his smile.

"You're going to pay for that smile, Ben. You know that, don't you?"

Ben chuckled. "I think your sister and I are going to be friends."

Lucien cursed and muttered under his breath for the rest of the journey, and Ben loved every minute. It was reassuring to know that he had an understanding ally in Maddy and that Lucien didn't always get things his own way.

* * * *

There were a few people hanging around the boathouse, racking boats and stowing gear. Seb must have left instructions because Ben often had to clear up after the morning session. They didn't have to wait for a boat and worked together to carry it down to the water. After a quick warm up, Ben spent forty-five minutes focused on nothing but the smooth motion of oars through the water. Lucien had such a consistent action that staying in time with him was easy. He set a tough pace but not so demanding that Ben couldn't keep up. Ben's aching muscles gradually unknotted and eased into the familiar movement. The synchronization of their bodies was effortless and Ben knew instinctively that they were a good pair. With training, they could be even better.

Returning to the boathouse, Lucien slowed, giving them both the chance to warm down.

"How are you doing?" he asked.

After getting over the shock of being asked, Ben glanced back. "I ache a bit from yesterday. I used some muscles that don't get exercised very often."

"Your general fitness level is high, but it needs to be even better if we're going to compete together."

"I'm not at your level, Lucien. Are you sure you want to pair up with me?" Ben was amazed that Lucien was considering competition.

"You could be, with some serious training, and yes, I am sure. You must see how well we fit together. Our styles are so similar."

The praise gave Ben a warm glow inside, which stayed with him as they disembarked and heaved the boat back to storage.

After a quick shower, Ben walked Lucien to his car.

"Can I trust you to behave yourself today?" Lucien ruffled Ben's hair and laughed as Ben ducked away from him.

"I'm so behind on my work that I'll be confined to a desk for the rest of the day. I have two assignments to finish and some reading prep to do—I suppose that makes you happy?"

"I don't like the idea of leaving you alone at all, but that's something I'm going to have to learn to live with, I suppose."

"There's not much I can get up to in lecture theaters or the library, Lucien. And what about you? Where will you be all day?"

"I've emailed you my schedule for the week and all the contact numbers you might need. I want you to do the same for me."

It took Ben a few seconds to realize that he was deadly serious. Nervous at taking the lead, he wrapped his arms around Lucien's body and kissed him softly.

"You can trust me. I promise."

Lucien's response was rough with desire, his kiss deep and hard. "If you weren't so beautiful... I don't want other men looking at you like I do."

Ben looked up into soft blue eyes. "You can't lock me away, Lucien. Looking isn't touching and I have no interest in anyone else."

"I should bloody well hope not. And locking you up is an interesting option—I might give it some consideration."

"Go to work and don't get too imaginative."

"Cheeky brat. I'll see you tonight."

Then he was gone, the car roaring away into the distance. Ben tried to push away the feelings of sadness and longing that immediately enveloped him.

He registered the feelings and stood stock still. "Fuck. I'm falling in love with him." Saying the words aloud made him realize they weren't quite true. "Fallen. Fallen in love. Bloody hell." So this is what it felt like. Confusing. Euphoric. Absolutely freaking terrifying.

It had never happened before. How the hell had he managed to pick such a complex man to fall in love with? He was beginning to see the multiple facets that made up Lucien Thorne, and physical attraction wasn't in question—the man was steaming hot. The question was whether he had it in him to love Ben back. The thought that he might not was unbearable, and something that Ben could only shove to the back of his mind, consigning the possibility to a dusty corner of his subconscious.

* * * *

Ben strolled back to the boathouse unseeing, totally wrapped up in his thoughts, so he didn't notice when Seb appeared from the locker room. He almost walked straight into him and pulled up short just in time.

"Watch where you're fucking going, Astor." Seb looked as if he was in the mood for a fight and Ben really didn't have the time or the energy for confrontation. He took a couple of steps back.

"I saw you with His Lordship this morning. I suppose you spent the weekend sucking his dick?"

"I spent the weekend working bloody hard, if you must know." Ben bridled at his tone.

"You don't know the meaning of the word 'work'. You can scrub all the floors today to make up for your slacking off."

"That'll take hours! I have to study. The only reason I wasn't here is because you insisted in putting me down for the promise auction."

"Please yourself. You can pack your stuff and move out instead, if you prefer."

"You can't do that." Ben shook with anger and frustration. Seb was a dick but he'd never threatened Ben's home before.

"Yes, I can. Of course, there is an alternative." He rubbed his groin suggestively and Ben thought he might throw up. "I'm sure that pretty mouth of yours is very talented."

"Fuck off, Seb!"

"Not good enough for you, is that it? I'd have thought a cocksucker like you would jump at the chance to get a mouthful of this." Seb was unzipping his fly, and Ben backed away in horror. Striking like a snake, Seb grabbed a handful of hair and pushed Ben to his knees. Ben twisted hard but couldn't get free. He could feel strands of hair ripping away. Seb was strong. He held Ben down with one hand and released his straining cock with the other, letting it slap into Ben's face.

"No!" Ben pulled away with all his strength, getting a hard backhand across the face in return. It was a small price to pay for being free of Seb's hold. Blood dripped from his nose and lip, but Ben didn't care as the fat red drops splattered the floor. He didn't know where to run. Seb had him boxed into a corner.

"Seb, where are you?" a female voice echoed from outside.

Seb blinked. "Coming!" He glared at Ben. "You won't be so lucky the next time I get you alone, Astor. Make sure you get the blood off when you scrub the floor." Then he calmly zipped up and sauntered toward daylight as if nothing had happened.

Ben sat shakily on the bottom of the stairs leading to his flat. Had that really just happened? He wiped the blood from his face and prodded at his swollen lip. There was no way he was going to be able to hide this from Lucien. He wasn't afraid to tell him, but he was afraid of what Lucien might do.

Numbly, he fetched a bucket of water and the scrubbing brush and began to clean the floors. The grinding monotony of the task calmed him down eventually as his emotions ran through a cycle of disgust, anger and shame.

* * * *

Four hours later, Ben mopped away the last suds and packed up the cleaning kit. His hands and knees were raw and bruised, but he felt as though Seb's touch had been washed away along with the grime on the floor. After a quick shower, he finally settled down to work. A quick peek at his email brought up the note from Lucien—terse and to the point. Attached was his calendar for the week and Ben looked at it, amazed at the number of meetings and appointments that seemed to fill Lucien's days. He shook his head. If Lucien could cope with so many demands on his time, then Ben should be able to manage a part-time job and a degree course.

He completed one of his assignments, an analysis of a particularly dull poem, and took a bathroom break. He threw some cold water over his face and made a critical examination of his reflection. The dull shadow of a bruise marked his cheekbone. His lip was swollen on one side, the cut a blackened line of dried blood. He probed at it gently, wincing at the pain. Seb hadn't held back.

What the hell pushed him over the edge like that? Something must be going on with him. What he did today constituted sexual assault. Ben shuddered. With no witnesses it was his word against Seb's. If he reported him it would just cause more trouble, and Ben couldn't afford to lose his home or his job. *I'll just have to make sure that he doesn't get me alone again.*

He made a coffee and settled back to work. The war poets would put Seb out of his head for a while at least.

* * * *

Ben barely noticed the time passing, but remembered to check the boathouse and open the main doors for the early evening rowers. There was no sign of Seb, thank goodness, and he got back to work as quickly as he could. By seven he had produced two essays that he was pleased with and had done the next week's worth of preparation. At least he would be able to attend tutorials and sound like he knew what he was talking about. He switched off his computer and sat back in his chair, flexing his aching fingers, wincing as his knuckles cracked.

The flat was dark apart from his small desk lamp — that meant it was time to lock up downstairs. It felt good to stretch and use muscles that had stiffened from sitting too long. He went down the stairs and sighed heavily at the mess the crews had left behind. He dealt with the boats first, racking and locking up carefully. In the locker room, he picked up discarded towels and hosed out the showers, closed locker doors and took out the trash.

He had already bolted the main doors, leaving just the access door to padlock. He nearly jumped out of his skin when it banged open, but to his relief it was Lucien ducking his head to get through the low opening. Relief was replaced by anxiety as Ben stepped into the light and watched Lucien's face freeze into an icy mask.

"What the fuck happened to you?" He gripped Ben's chin and turned his head from side to side. "Never mind. Get upstairs. Now." He took the keys from Ben's hand and locked the small door before following him up to the flat.

"Sit."

Ben balanced nervously on the edge of a chair while Lucien rummaged in the kitchen and produced a bottle of wine that Ben had been chilling in the fridge, and two glasses. He handed over a brimming glass, then took a long swallow of his own.

"One day. I leave you alone for one day."

"Promise me you won't do anything stupid and I'll tell you what happened."

"You'll tell me anyway. No promises."

Ben sighed, but in a halting voice told Lucien everything. He left nothing out. When he'd finished Lucien's eyes had darkened to the color of flint, his expression brittle with fury.

"Explain to me why you didn't ring me immediately, Benedict."

Ben cast his eyes down. "I didn't want to bother you at work. He was gone and I was okay. It's just a few bruises."

His hands were shaking. Lucien spotted them and seemed immediately contrite. He lifted Ben's head with a finger under his chin. "I'm sorry. I'm mad at Seb—I shouldn't be taking it out on you." The kiss that followed was hard and reproving. "That doesn't mean that I won't be punishing you a little later."

Ben flushed and gave a shy smile. "Just a little?"

Lucien shook his head and rolled his eyes. "I was going to suggest we go out to eat, but I don't want to be accused of slapping you around. Do you have anything edible in the place?"

"Eggs, cheese… I make a really good omelet. I have stuff for a salad."

"Perfect. Dealing with Seb can wait until tomorrow. I don't know what's going on in his head, but he is seriously screwed."

Ben took what he needed from the fridge. He cracked eggs into a bowl and whisked. "This place isn't much, Lucien, but I need it and my job."

"I'm a lawyer, Ben. There are plenty of ways of dealing with scum like Seb that don't involve physical violence, tempting though that would be. He has no right to touch you, threaten you or force you to work outside of your contracted hours. You do have a contract of some kind?"

"Yes, I can show you the paperwork. I'm not the first person to have this job, it's an ongoing thing."

"I admit, despite being a club member for some time, I've never noticed anyone care taking the place before you," Lucien said.

Ben stirred grated cheese into the beaten egg then added some chopped chives. He poured the mixture into a hot pan. Lucien prepared a side salad and they worked side by side.

"He's never been so…direct before. He's always been a bully, but I never dreamed he would do something like this."

After a couple of minutes stirring and flipping, he cut the omelet in half and slid the pieces onto two plates. Lucien heaped salad onto side plates. They carried the food across to the couch then sat with their plates on their knees.

"I think there's something else going on with him."

Lucien paused, a forkful of food halfway to his mouth. "You amaze me. After what he did to you, you should be cursing his name, not analyzing his motivation."

"Maybe I just hope that there's a shred of good in everyone."

Lucien raised a dark eyebrow. "Does that include me?"

"There's no hope for you." Ben hid his smile just a little too late.

They ate in companionable silence but as soon as Lucien had finished his last mouthful, he walked across the room and bolted the door. "Are you finished?" His tone was full of menace. "I want you naked, on your knees, in thirty seconds."

Ben's eyes widened as his cock reacted to the words with an enthusiastic jerk. "No! You can't..."

"Make you? I think I can. Now do as you're told. Every ten seconds you make me wait is one slap across that beautiful arse of yours."

Ben didn't know what to do. He was so turned on it hurt, but he wasn't fulfilling a promise now. This was another step down a path that he was still terrified of following.

"Benedict. Knees. Naked. Now. Is anything unclear to you?"

Lucien didn't move. He didn't need to. There was no part of him that didn't emanate the expectation of absolute obedience. Ben made eye contact and realized that there was nothing to be afraid of—he saw no cruelty, only naked desire. Slowly, and with trembling hands, he stripped to his shorts and watched as Lucien's gaze roamed his body.

"Help me?" The whispered words spoke volumes and Lucien instantly understood. A couple of short steps and he stroked Ben's smooth, warm skin. Before Ben realized what was happening, his shorts were around his ankles and Lucien's hands were on his arse, then squeezing his balls, then tormenting his cock. He gasped, fighting with every ounce of willpower to keep still.

Lucien unbuckled his belt and slid it from its loops. "Down."

Ben dropped to his hands and knees, his heart pounding. How could he be so excited and petrified at the same time? He parted his legs and raised his arse in the air, moaning as the belt slapped gently against his hanging cock and balls. He desperately wanted to touch himself but didn't dare, and when the belt slashed across his arse he was glad he was balancing on both hands.

"You made me wait for nearly a minute, Benedict. I'll give you the benefit of the doubt as I'm feeling generous, and go with five strokes instead of six."

The belt landed again and Ben yelped as a line of fire seared his skin. It felt so good, and he writhed shamelessly, his cock throbbing. By the fifth lash he was panting with need, the pain fading rapidly to a hot glow.

"Touch yourself and you get five more."

Lucien moved to stand in front of him and unfastened the button on his waistband.

"On your knees."

His fly strained and Ben reached up to pull the zip down.

"No!" Lucien took off his tie and used it to restrain Ben's hands behind his back.

Shocked, Ben struggled against the bindings but the knots held fast.

"That's better. Now try again. Don't give me that hurt puppy look, Benedict. Get to work."

With a bit of effort, Ben managed to lower the zip using his teeth. To his delight, Lucien wasn't wearing underwear. His thick length sprang forward and Ben caught the moist tip with his tongue as it passed. He watched, mesmerized, as it settled into stillness.

Ignoring the ache of his bruised knees, he shuffled into a better position and took Lucien's length deep into his throat. He pulled back, grazing sensitive skin with his teeth as he went. That brought a growl from Lucien's throat, and he twisted his hands, which had been gently stroking Ben's hair, firmly into the strands and pulled.

"Behave."

Lips and tongue and teeth became Ben's weapons as he tormented Lucien's cock with swirling licks and powerful suction.

"Fuck!" Lucien could hold back no longer — he jerked his hips and pulled Ben's head closer, fucking his mouth and throat over and over again. Helpless with his hands bound, Ben was overwhelmed by the taste and scent of him, and when Lucien began to pull away he leaned into him, accepting the final thrust and warm flow that followed with delight. Licking his lips, he looked up anxiously for signs of pleasure and satisfaction. Lucien's eyes were bright as he pulled him to his feet so that they were almost eye to eye, then Ben felt the warmth of Lucien's hand around his cock turn into the intense heat of friction as Lucien jerked him faster and faster. His balls contracted, then he exploded into an orgasm that made his legs shake so much that he had to lean against Lucien for support. Lucien wrapped his arm around Ben, and whispered words that reassured him. Gently, Lucien guided him to the edge of the bed and untied his hands.

"Sit down and rest. I'll get some drinks."

As he fetched more wine, Lucien kept looking back as if he couldn't let go with his eyes. Ben smiled shyly and pulled the quilt around his shoulders. He could feel the marks of the belt on his arse, taste Lucien in his mouth, and he knew that he wanted more. He wanted Lucien to throw him down and take him right there. He wanted to feel Lucien's weight pinning him, holding him down. He wanted the burn of aggressive penetration, the thrust of powerful hips. He had imagined so many times how it would feel…

He was startled from his daydream by the sound of breaking glass. He glanced across to Lucien, but there were still two wine goblets on the table and the bottle was in his hand.

"What was that?"

Lucien put a finger to his lips and gestured for silence.

"Downstairs. Someone's in the boathouse." His whisper barely registered as he moved silently toward the door and snicked the lock open as quietly as he could.

Hurriedly, Ben began to dress. Lucien, who only had to zip up his trousers, was already out of the door and heading downstairs, and Ben didn't want him down there alone. He hopped into his trousers, didn't bother with a shirt or shoes and followed Lucien as quickly and quietly as he could. As he neared the bottom stair he heard scuffling, a muffled curse, then the sounds of someone running.

"Stop!" Lucien's voice echoed through the large open space as he shot after the intruder, almost tripping through the small access door. The two figures hurtled down the path toward the river and Ben followed quickly but cautiously — he could see the glint of broken glass on the floor. Outside, he began to run toward the water, careless of the rocks and stones beneath his feet. There was no time to be wary anymore as he watched Lucien tear toward the water in pursuit of a dark figure a few feet in front of him. There was a cry and a loud splash as someone fell headlong into the river. Ben got to the bank just in time to see Lucien dive in. For a few anxious moments, Ben stared into the darkness then, to his relief, Lucien broke the surface, pulling another body with him. Ben clambered down the muddy bank and helped pull the second man up the slope onto the grass as Lucien crawled out and flopped down, exhausted.

"Fuck, that water's cold." He coughed a little, spat out some river water and sat up. His downed quarry was flat on his face, moaning into the mud. Lucien shoved him over and swore. "Seb! Fuck, if I'd known it was you I'd have left you in the river."

"Screw you, Thorne." Seb heaved himself up and sat with his head between his knees, gasping for breath.

Lucien shoved him down on his back again. "I'd be very careful about your next move, Seb. You assaulted my boyfriend earlier today and I'm not in the best of moods."

"Boyfriend? Who…? You mean Astor? You must be fucking desperate." Water from Seb's dripping hair ran down his face like tears.

"That's it. I'm throwing you back in." Lucien took hold of Seb's soaking shirt and heaved him toward the water.

"No! All right, I'm sorry!" Seb started choking and glared at him.

"What the hell were you doing? Breaking into the trophy cabinet?"

"It's not what it looks like…"

"It looks like breaking and entering. A criminal offense. You owe us a bloody good explanation."

Warily, Seb sat up again and caught sight of Ben, shirtless and shivering.

"Did I interrupt something?"

Lucien cuffed him around the head. "Get your eyes away from him and tell me what's going on."

"Don't hit me!" Seb cowered, his hands over his head. "I'll tell you. I was after the trophies but wasn't going to keep them. I was going to hide them and claim on the insurance."

"Are you that desperate for money? Why don't you just ask Mummy Dearest, she isn't short of a few quid?"

"You don't understand. I lost a bet... I was drunk... There's no way I could go to Mother, she'd disinherit me."

"What did you lose, Seb?" Ben asked. "It has to be something major to drive you to this."

"The boathouse. I bet the deeds to the boathouse." Seb hid his face in his hands.

"Unbelievable. You fucking idiot." Lucien cuffed Seb's head again. "Who did you lose them to?"

"Who do you think? I was playing poker with Cecil Carrington and a few of his cronies. They invited me to a private game. There was so much champagne and they were really nice to me."

"Cecil Carrington? Club president of our biggest rivals, Thamesmead?"

Seb nodded. Lucien groaned, and Ben cursed under his breath. Thamesmead and Okeanos had been head to head so many times, the two rowing clubs were notorious for their enmity.

"Cecil said he would give me the deeds back if I found ten grand by the end of the week. Some of those trophies are solid silver, they're worth a mint."

"Call the police, Ben," Lucien said, "while I have a quiet word with our idiot friend here. He and I have a few things to discuss."

Ben jogged back inside. He didn't look back. He didn't want to know what Lucien was doing to Seb. *He deserves everything he gets, but a little bit of me pities him. I have Lucien. He has nothing but problems and nowhere to hide.*

* * * *

Ben made his call and within half an hour the blue light of a police car lit up the riverbank. Lucien had taken Seb back inside to the scene of the crime, and he sat against the wall with a towel wrapped around his shoulders, looking about as miserable and dejected as it was possible to be.

There were two policemen—a gruff, burly sergeant and a much younger constable who Lucien thought didn't look much older than Ben. He had sandy hair, freckles and light green eyes that darted constantly around. They introduced themselves as Sergeant Alf Shaw and PC Rick Dennison. PC Dennison was ordered to take notes while the sergeant asked the questions.

The young PC's eyes constantly drifted from his notebook to Ben's unbuttoned shirt, which he had hastily thrown on while he made the phone call. Ben was completely oblivious to the attention but Lucien wasn't.

"Ben, would you mind making some tea while we go through this. I'm bloody freezing and a hot drink would help thaw me out. I suppose you'd better make one for this idiot as well." He gestured at Seb. "I don't want him dying from hypothermia before he's arrested."

"Sure, no problem." Ben seemed glad to have something to do. "Sergeant, would you and the constable like a hot drink?"

"Tea would go down a treat. Milk and three sugars please," Sergeant Shaw said.

"Just milk for me, please." PC Dennison gave Ben a beaming smile.

As Ben disappeared up the stairs, Lucien's gaze drilled into the young PC, and he went very pale beneath the freckles. He became very focused on his notebook.

It didn't take long to get the whole story out of Seb. His whole demeanor seemed to have shrunk in the last half an hour. He had little choice but to admit to the break-in, having been caught virtually red-handed. The sergeant took some details from Lucien about what he had heard and how they had both ended up in the river. Ben came back with a tray of tea, including two mugs for the policemen, and volunteered his own version of events.

When it was all down in writing, the sergeant slurped his tea and cast an amused glance at his colleague, who was trying, unsuccessfully, not to drool in Ben's direction.

"So, Mr. Thorne—sorry, Your Lordship. Just to clarify, you and Mr. Astor are...?"

"He's my boyfriend, Sergeant. Is that relevant?"

Lucien glared at PC Dennison rather than his boss. The sergeant chuckled. "Just ensuring we don't have any misunderstandings. Dennison! Scrape your fucking tongue off the floor and go start up the car before you end up in the river as well!"

The young PC gave his boss a sheepish look. "Thanks for the tea," he muttered before strolling out into the night.

Seb was led away in handcuffs and the sergeant promised to keep in touch with any developments.

Lucien turned to Ben. "Unbelievable. You're not safe even around policemen!"

Ben looked totally bewildered. "What did I do?"

"That's the problem. You don't even notice when someone's looking at you like they want to jump you there and then."

"Who? The sergeant?"

"Oh, for fuck's sake. Get upstairs, Benedict."

As soon as they were inside the flat, Lucien stripped all his clothes off and stood, stark naked, in front of the wood burner. Backlit by the glow of the fire, he rubbed his cold limbs as Ben stared, entranced.

"A bathrobe or towel would be nice, Ben."

"Oh! Sorry…" Ben fetched his robe and handed it over, disappointed that Lucien would be able to hide his magnificent body. To his surprise, Lucien pulled him close and wrapped him in it too. He rested his head on Lucien's shoulder and kissed his neck.

"I should be so pissed off at you. Tackling burglars alone in the dark, jumping in the bloody river… What if you had been hurt?"

Lucien hugged him tightly. "You're not allowed to tell me off, Ben. It's the other way round, remember?"

Ben struggled free and took a step back. "I'm serious, you stubborn idiot."

"Ben, I'm fine. I'm sorry I scared you." His lips twitched. "Did you just call me a stubborn idiot?"

Ben nodded and took a step back.

"I thought so. And your arse must be pretty sore already…"

"Stay away from me, you sadist. My arse is off limits!"

"Really? You're mine, remember. Mine to do with as I wish, when I wish. Aren't you?"

Ben chewed on his lower lip, winced as he caught the cut there, and said nothing.

"Tell me!"

Ben's heart pounded. Lucien looked gloriously stern and forbidding, and he loved him all the more for it.

"Yes." His voice was soft and faltering. "Yours."

Lucien folded his arms across his chest. "Take those trousers off—they look wet." He shrugged off the robe and dropped it to the floor, revealing a rigid, twitching erection. "Then I think it's time I did something about your virginity, don't you?"

Chapter Twelve

"Don't look so worried, Benedict. It's not doing my ego any good at all." Lucien crossed the room in a few strides and wrapped Ben in his arms. "We take this at your pace, okay? I'm not going to do anything to hurt you. I promise."

Ben trembled within his embrace and melted against him.

"Sorry, it's just... I never thought this would happen with someone like you."

"Like me?" Lucien rubbed Ben's back in slow circles.

"Someone I care about."

"I dread to think how you imagined giving yourself to someone for the first time then."

"I don't know. I suppose I had all these romantic dreams but as I got older they became tinged with a healthy dose of reality. Drunken fumbling with another inexperienced student probably. I'm glad it's not like that." He nuzzled against Lucien's solid chest.

"You're shaking."

"Sorry, I'm a little nervous.

"Stop apologizing. Let's take a shower. I need to get the smell of the river off me and you need to relax."

Ben didn't resist as he was towed toward the tiny bathroom. Lucien turned the spray on and gave a deep laugh as it sputtered into life.

"This is by far the worst shower I have ever come across."

The humor helped Ben's nerves considerably.

"The water coming out of it is clear not brown. I consider that a win."

The water was hot, if not that consistent, and soon the room filled with steam. Lucien placed his hands gently around Ben's waist.

"Okay?" He waited for Ben's nod before unfastening his trousers and pushing them down.

Ben held his breath. The lightest touch of Lucien's fingers on his arse made him whimper and clench his muscles. His skin felt so sensitive, and he longed for Lucien to touch him more intimately. His aching cock throbbed and he took a step closer to Lucien so that it made contact with the man's hardness. Slowly, Ben swiveled his hips and their bodies rubbed together. It was having some effect, because Lucien's fingers spasmed and dug into the flesh of his arse, locking their bodies together.

"Keep doing that and I might just shove you up against the wall and take you here and now." He took a step back into the shower. "Get in here, brat."

There wasn't a huge amount of room in the cubicle. Lucien grasped Ben's hips and turned him around to face the wall. He lathered his hands with scented gel and gently began to massage it into Ben's shoulders, slowly encouraging the tension to dissipate from his knotted muscles. He soaped Ben's back and smoothed the suds down to the jutting curve of his arse before shifting his attention to his chest and stomach. He continued stroking and kneading until Ben could bear it no more.

"Touch me, Lucien, please!"

"I think I'm already doing that, aren't I?"

"You know what I mean!"

Lucien moved his hands lower, giving the briefest brush to Ben's slippery cock. He concentrated his fleeting touches on the join between Ben's hip and thigh, then stroked his upper legs.

Frantic, Ben pushed back against him, grinding his hips shamelessly. Lucien gave a low chuckle and slicked more gel onto his hands, then slipped one finger between Ben's soapy cheeks to circle his small rosebud entrance while he massaged Ben's balls with his other hand.

"Oh God, Lucien, I'm going to come."

"No. You're not."

At the very point of orgasm, Lucien withdrew both hands. "That's enough." He shoved the gel into Ben's shaking hand. "Your turn."

Ben turned around with a frustrated moan. "You bastard."

Lucien kissed him hard, biting his lip and drawing blood. "You think pushing me is a good idea, Ben? Just give me an excuse…"

Ben lowered his eyes and focused on soaping Lucien's broad chest. Free rein to run his hands over all that solid muscle was a joy, but did little to alleviate the tight burn of his balls. He let his hands roam, sliding them across slick, smooth skin, gradually working lower until he could slip his fingers around Lucien's narrow hips and work on his arse.

They were face to face, and Lucien pulled him close so their cocks rubbed together. He grabbed Ben's arms to still his hands and thrust one knee between his legs, forcing them apart. Silently he bore down on him, his slight extra height allowing him to assert some force. Ben jerked and moaned, helpless in Lucien's grip.

"Is this how you want it, Ben? Do you want to be taken?" Lucien whispered in his ear. "Tell me how you dreamed this would be." He twisted Ben around and pushed him aggressively against the wet tiles, probing one slippery digit between arse cheeks that tensed at his touch.

Ben cried out as Lucien penetrated the outer ring of his defenses and slid into him to the second knuckle.

"Oh, it burns. Feels good."

"Tell me what you want, Ben."

"I want you to force me, Lucien, hold me down and… Aagh!"

Lucien twisted his finger inside Ben and touched something that temporarily blinded him with sensation.

"Are you sure?" *That whisper again…* "There's no going back if you say yes."

Ben was having trouble staying upright, let alone thinking coherently, but he managed to spit out the words, "I'm sure!"

Lucien turned off the shower. Lucien grabbed a handful of Ben's locks and shoved him out of the shower. Water streamed from their hair and bodies. His finger slid free and Ben moaned at the loss, but the sensation was soon replaced by a firm grip on his cock as Lucien dragged him out of the bathroom toward the bed. Lucien really did throw him down, and seconds later his weight pressed down against Ben's back. A couple of firm slaps across his wet arse shocked him into a state of acute awareness, and he tried to struggle as Lucien used a belt to tie his hands to the headboard.

His own hardness was trapped beneath him, then Lucien pulled his cock and balls back to lie between his legs, touching and squeezing, driving him wild with need.

The torment seemed to last forever, and it took Ben a while to realize that Lucien had got up and was rummaging in his overnight bag. Ben's hands were tied in such a way that he couldn't free himself, but he could turn over, so he twisted onto his back. The leather around his wrists dug in hard, but it was worth it to try to see what Lucien was up to.

Lucien stood and loomed over him, dark hair falling across his eyes. "I don't remember saying you could move, Benedict. You need to learn that there are consequences for exerting free will around me."

He climbed across Ben's hips and rested his weight across his thighs, pinning him down. He didn't say anything, but held a small strip of studded leather in front of Ben's startled eyes so that he could see it. Attached to the band was a slim silver chain that divided into a Y shape and ended with two vicious-looking clamps.

Lucien buckled the leather strap around the base of Ben's cock. The studs were on the inside, pressing hard into his flesh as Lucien tightly fastened the strap. Ben's moans increased as the cool silver chain trailed across his abdomen and the rubber-tipped clamps rested lightly on his chest. Lucien bent down and sucked each nipple in turn, biting gently until each rosy nub peaked into hardness.

"You loved these so much the first time. Attaching the chain to your cock ring adds a whole new dimension."

Ben writhed as his lover attached the clamps. The pressure was intense and sent an immediate burn to his dick, which jerked in response. As it did, the fine chain was tugged, pulling on his tender nipples and starting the cycle again. Lucien began to massage his balls, causing him to twist and squirm, each movement causing more pain to his tortured nipples.

The agony was exquisite and Ben was so close to coming that his vision blurred. He lifted his knees slightly to relieve the tension on the chain and Lucien grinned.

"That's right, straight into my trap. Nice and exposed for me."

"Oh Christ, Lucien, please! I need you." Ben's cock head was slick with need and he was a panting, incoherent mess of emotion. He would have continued to beg if he thought it would do any good but even through a fog of lust he understood that Lucien would do exactly as he wanted.

Lucien made a show of slicking two fingers with lube and thrust them into Ben's channel. The scream that followed as he twisted his hand, scissoring and stretching, just seemed to encourage him to thrust harder.

"Fuck, fuck, fuck..." Ben's voice was strained and tight. His arse burned, inside and out. He felt Lucien's fingers inside him, his knuckles pushing into the sides of his channel. He pulled his knees back farther and spread his legs apart, feeling like a complete slut but helpless to do anything else. When Lucien withdrew Ben could have sobbed, but a couple of tweaks to the chain attached to his cock strap had stars exploding behind his eyes.

He was hardly aware of Lucien sheathing himself in rubber or slicking his cock with lube, but the instant his resistant ring of muscle was breached he came with a scream as burning pain and intense pleasure competed for his attention. Lucien had no mercy. He took Ben at his word and pistoned in and out of his arse, powered by thigh muscles conditioned by years of rowing. Ben writhed beneath him, bound arms stretched, every muscle straining, tears running down his face even as he tried to shove himself harder onto Lucien's cock.

"So good. Harder." Ben couldn't manage any more words but for once it was Lucien obeying an order.

With one last powerful thrust, Lucien came. He spasmed again and again. His fingers ground into Ben's hips. His weight pushed Ben back almost double, and as Lucien's balls drained themselves with a final gush, he leaned forward and penetrated Ben's mouth with his tongue, possessing him utterly.

Lucien replaced his bruising lips and tongue with his hand, gagging Ben firmly. He stared down at him with frightening intensity. "Now you are truly mine. No one ever gets to touch you but me, do you understand?"

Beneath the pressure of his hand, Ben nodded, his eyes full of tears. Maintaining the pressure across his mouth, Lucien knelt up, his cock sliding free of Ben's channel. He used his other hand to release the nipple clamps and grinned as Ben arched beneath him and tried to scream. The pain was fiery, intense and inescapable. With an evil chuckle worthy of any B-movie villain, Lucien took away the hand gag and ground both thumbs into Ben's swollen, tender buds.

Ben bucked frantically beneath him, tears pouring from his eyes as the burn increased. He yanked hard against his bonds but could do nothing to escape as Lucien probed inside him once again. Ben fought so hard he thought his wrists might dislocate. Lucien had two—no, three fingers inside him and the other hand was now tugging on his semi-hard dick. Lucien squeezed the studded cock strap before rubbing Ben's perineum.

"You see how it is, Ben, don't you? This torture continues until I decide it stops. Nothing you can do or say will change that." Lucien said the words with absolute certainty, smiling down at his victim. "Now, fucking turn over."

Hard again, Lucien didn't hesitate before rolling on a fresh condom and ramming his claim home once more, digging his nails into Ben's arse. Ben was sore from the belt lashes he had taken earlier, but he welcomed the pain and relished Lucien's strength as his lover pushed down on Ben's lower back and slammed into his channel.

Ben tore into the pillow with his teeth, cursing Lucien's name even as he begged for him to move harder, faster. Every sensitive part of him was alive with sensation and as Lucien released for the second time, Ben bucked his hips up and came too before collapsing, exhausted, into the tangle of damp sheets.

"I think you killed me, but fuck, what a way to go."

Lucien snorted. "You're very much alive, sweetheart, and you'll be feeling me for days to prove it."

Ben giggled. "You have impressive recovery time."

"I had excellent motivation, though you might have to wait a while for round three."

Slowly and deliberately, Lucien withdrew from Ben's body. Ben appreciated the care. His arse ached deliciously. He experienced a pang of loss when Lucien left him and went to the bathroom to deal with the condom and clean up. When he returned, Ben was still flat on his stomach, arms stretched painfully over his head. He had deep grooves in his wrists where he had fought the belt restraining him and he smelled of sweat and cum. Lucien had marked him with his scent, bruised him, taken him in every way possible. Lucien looked down at him and smiled. Ben flushed at the possessive look and felt a deep swell of love burning through his system.

Lucien removed the cock strap first, then released the belt from around Ben's wrists. He massaged the sore skin tenderly, then rolled Ben onto his back, brushing tendrils of hair from his face. Ben felt like those blue eyes were piercing his soul, exposing his innermost feelings, and before he could stop himself the words slipped from his lips. "I love you, Lucien."

Lucien had obviously expected to be cursed and sworn at. He was so completely knocked off balance that it showed all over his face. Everything hard and unyielding about him melted away, and for once he seemed speechless. Ben sat up shakily and flung his arms around the man he knew, with absolute certainty, he loved more than anything in the world.

His embrace was returned—harder, stronger, so tightly it hurt. When the words came, whispered so softly in his ear, Ben sobbed with joy. "I love you too, Ben, more than I ever thought possible."

They kissed, gently then with determined passion, lost in each other for long moments before slowly drawing apart. Their eyes met and Ben's stomach knotted with fear. He couldn't lose Lucien—not now, not ever, and God, how he hoped Lucien felt the same.

Chapter Thirteen

Ben slept better than he had in weeks, curled into the curve of Lucien's body, but it felt as though his eyes had only just closed when the alarm went off at five-thirty the next morning. For a while he lay there, acknowledging the aches in various parts of his body, and a slow, lazy smile spread across his face. Lucien grunted and tightened his arm around Ben's waist.

"Keep still. You wriggle too much."

"I have to go to work, Lucien… I need to clear up the broken glass from the trophy cabinet before the crews arrive, remember?"

"Fuck." Lucien's voice was rough with sleep. "I had other plans for you this morning."

Ben winced at the thought and felt grateful for his job for the first time ever. "Go back to sleep. I'll open up the boathouse and come to wake you up again in a couple of hours."

Lucien began stroking the curve of his arse, and Ben's morning erection stiffened.

"I hope you're not too sore to row?" Lucien's touch moved dangerously close to Ben's hole.

"Nothing some anesthetic and a cushion won't deal with." Ben pulled gently away, and this time Lucien grudgingly let him go.

"Sorry?"

"That has to be the least sincere apology I've ever heard." Ben chuckled as Lucien rolled onto his front and buried his head in the pillow. He leaned down and planted a kiss on Lucien's bare shoulder. "You gave me exactly what I wanted. Don't be sorry."

Lucien tilted his head to the side and opened one eye. "Either get your cute little arse back into bed, Ben, or go to work. Stop tormenting me with what I can't have."

Ben kissed the end of his nose. Lucien growled.

Reluctantly, Ben pulled on his rowing gear and padded across to the kitchen area. He drank a quick glass of orange juice and poured one for Lucien who, by the time Ben turned around, was sitting up in bed with a supremely satisfied look on his handsome face. Ben drank in the sight of his broad chest and almost decided that he could bear a little more pain, but the clock was his master this morning.

"Aren't you going to have a lie in?"

"I'm an early riser." Lucien smirked at the double meaning.

Ben rolled his eyes. He put the glass of juice down next to the bed. "I really have to go." It was so hard to drag himself away.

Lucien smiled. "I'm not stopping you, Ben. You're free to go." He stretched, allowing the covers to shift low enough to reveal his thick cock, ramrod straight and glistening. Lucien ran his tongue across his lower lip. He wrapped his fingers around the rigid length of his dick and hummed as he stroked himself slowly. Ben cursed and ran for the door, blocking Lucien's deep, sexy chuckle from his ears.

Ben cleared up the broken glass from the trophy cabinet and gave the floor a thorough sweeping. Tiny shards of glass had scattered far and wide and the last thing he wanted was for Seb to cause more grief by causing an injury. He had to knock the remainder of the glass from the cabinet door because it was lethally jagged, and he wondered whether he ought to move all the trophies upstairs to his flat. Maybe Lucien's sister had a safe where the most valuable ones could be stored for a while. By the time he opened the main doors to the boathouse and removed the padlocks and chains from the boats, people were starting to arrive. It was only a few minutes before the first person noticed the missing glass and soon the club was buzzing with news of the attempted burglary. Ben just said that the robber had been interrupted and that the police had caught him. He didn't mention Lucien's chase or dive into the river, nor did he name Seb as the culprit. The news would filter out soon enough. He was touched by the number of people who asked if he was okay, knowing that he lived above the boathouse, but the attention made him uncomfortable and he ended up half hiding behind the boat racks.

Lucien came down the stairs, attempting — and failing miserably — to look innocent. Ben wanted to be cross with him but couldn't look at him without feeling a warm glow inside. He still couldn't believe that the word 'love' had come from those fierce lips, but it had. Twice the previous day, he'd been referred to openly as someone's boyfriend — something that had never happened before. Lucien was so brave. Ben had never hidden his sexuality, but his shyness meant that he hadn't broadcast it, either. He still suffered whispered abuse and occasional open hostility, but knew better than to rise to the taunts. Lucien had the advantage of money, a forceful personality and a title—Ben couldn't imagine him taking crap from anyone.

"Are you going to stand there daydreaming all morning, Benedict, or do you think you can summon up the energy to row?" Lucien pulled him from his hiding place.

Ben sighed. For once, he wasn't looking forward to sitting on that hard, narrow seat.

"You don't seem particularly enthused about rowing this morning, Ben." Lucien smirked.

"How can you be so fresh and perky after a few hours sleep? You didn't even take advantage of a lie-in."

"I found the night's activities...rejuvenating. Did you just refer to me as perky?"

Ben decided that it was best not to answer that question. "We'd better get going, there's only one double left."

"Perky. No fucking way. Studly I'd accept at a pinch."

Ben fell about laughing.

"Get your end of the boat, Benedict. I predict a very tough session this morning."

Ben groaned. "You should be going easy on me. You're the cause of my discomfort!"

They hoisted the boat above their heads and walked it out.

"One thing you can be sure of is that I will never, ever go easy on you. You wouldn't like it if I did."

Ben poked his tongue out at Lucien's back.

"Someone's earning himself a spanking."

Ben gaped. "How did you...?"

"Dom's intuition."

Ben had no answer to that. He hefted his end of the boat and increased his stride to keep up with Lucien.

* * * *

An hour later, Ben was calling Lucien all kinds of names under his breath as they carried the double scull back to the boathouse. On the return journey it weighed three times as much, adding to Ben's misery. His muscles ached so much that he was convinced that first-hand experience of a medieval torture rack couldn't have been any worse. Lucien had set such a hard pace that Ben had wondered what he had done wrong—it felt like punishment, not exercise. "He'd have made a bloody good inquisitor," Ben muttered under his breath. His ideal day would be spent soaking in a hot tub for about three hours, then sleeping for the next twenty-four. However, they both had busy days ahead, though Lucien was a little vague about what exactly that would involve on his part. Ben had a tutorial and several lectures.

Once they'd stowed the boat, Lucien threw a sweatshirt on over his rowing gear.

"I need to go home and collect some papers, so I'm going to shower and change there. Showering with you would just result in me being late for my first meeting."

"And punctuality is very important."

Ben's emotions hovered between disappointment that Lucien wasn't trying to tempt him back into bed and relief that his sore arse didn't have to take any more abuse. He accompanied Lucien to the car park where Lucien spun him around and pushed him against the Aston.

"Be good. I'll call you later."

Ben was expecting a chaste goodbye kiss, what he got was a breathtaking, lust generating, ravishment of his mouth that left him sagging, weak-kneed, against the car. A few whistles and slow clapping came from some of the other rowers along with the obligatory 'Get a room!' comment.

"I've made you blush." Lucien stroked Ben's cheek.

"You almost made me come!" Ben whispered urgently.

"My work here is done." Lucien gave him a final, gentle kiss then drove away, leaving Ben to tackle the walk back to the boathouse attempting to hide his erection.

Ben drifted through the remainder of the morning in a haze of happiness, but gradually, as time went on, he began to dissect every moment of the previous night and started to panic that he had given away his feelings too soon. He hadn't been able to stop himself. Lucien had taken his virginity in a way that had fulfilled all his most erotic dreams. It was as if he had known exactly what had been going on in Ben's mind and every minute, every second, had deepened Ben's feelings.

He had never intended to admit that he was in love, and now he was terrified that Lucien's response had just been reaction rather than heartfelt. He'd probably never see him again—a man like him would run a mile rather than tie himself down. Ben's fevered imagination constructed every scenario of rejection and abandonment possible, and by mid-afternoon he was convinced that Lucien would want nothing more to do with him. The logical part of his brain told him he was being ridiculous, the emotional part tortured him with doubt and insecurity.

At three o'clock Ben packed away the books he'd been staring at for the better part of two hours without absorbing a word. A quick glance out of the window revealed that the mild autumn morning had undergone a psychotic weather makeover and rain pounded from a purple-gray sky. Ben groaned. With no car and no public transport available, the cycle ride to university along the river path was his only option.

Ben arrived at his tutor's study sopping wet and miserable. He felt queasy and distracted. It wasn't the best state of mind to be in when meeting with Professor Ellis. The man had a well-deserved reputation as an utter shit, and had been known to rip essays up and toss them out of his study window. Ben had felt the sharp lash of his tongue on several occasions, but hadn't experienced his work being torn up in front of his eyes. Ellis had been his tutor for two years, and though Ben was a little afraid of him, he also respected him. The man was brilliant, insightful and unlike some professors, took time to get to know the students he tutored.

Ben knocked on the door and waited for the gruff, "Come in," that followed before entering Professor Ellis' sanctum. There were much larger offices in the English faculty building, but Ellis occupied a prime corner position with two high windows. On one side he had a view of the quad, on the other the vista was open fields with the river in the distance. Bookcases lined the walls and a familiar smell of leather and old paper immediately made Ben feel at home. The professor wasn't sitting behind his enormous, leather-topped desk, but in one of two armchairs next to the window. On a low table at his knee stood a teapot, milk jug and two mugs. Ben twisted his hips and contorted his body to get into the second chair. It was worth the effort as he sank into deep, squashy cushions.

"Good morning, Mr. Astor. Thank you for gracing me with your presence. I believe you are two minutes late?"

"I apologize, sir." In their very first meeting three years earlier, Ben hadn't known what to call his new tutor. The professor hadn't seemed to be the type to use first names as many of the other academic staff did, and he still remembered the sharp, 'Sir will do, boy. For pity's sake, stop hovering and sit.'

"No lame excuses, then. That, at least, is to your credit. Would you care to explain why you are making damp patches on my furniture?"

"I just cycled in along the river, sir. It's raining rather heavily."

"'Let the rain kiss you. Let the rain beat upon your head with silver liquid drops. Let the rain sing you a lullaby.' Who wrote that, Mr. Astor?"

"Um, Langston Hughes, sir. American poet."

"Indeed. Very good. He also wrote, 'Hold fast to dreams, for if dreams die, life is a broken-winged bird that cannot fly.' Something for you to bear in mind." Professor Ellis got up and retrieved a towel from a holdall next to his desk.

"I have a date to play squash later. This is clean." He handed over the towel, and Ben mopped at his face and hair. He'd left his raincoat in the men's room and his clothes had stayed relatively dry beneath its protection. He was only waterlogged from the neck up and thighs down.

Professor Ellis pressed a mug of tea into his hands. "Drink this." The professor resumed his seat and picked up his own mug.

Ben stifled a snort at the slogan printed on the side — *I would challenge you to a battle of wits, but I see you are unarmed.* William Shakespeare. He certainly didn't relish the prospect of engaging in any kind of intellectual battle with Professor Ellis, he knew when he was outgunned.

Professor Ellis leaned toward him. "Is that a bruise on your face? Has someone hurt you?" His voice was cold and hard.

"There was an…incident, at the boathouse. It's been dealt with, sir. I'm fine."

Ellis' expression was skeptical. "You can come to me any time if you need to talk, Benedict."

"Yes, sir. Thank you. I'm fine, really." *God, please change the subject.* Ben fidgeted in his seat.

Apparently satisfied for the moment, the professor picked up a file and pulled Ben's two most recent essays from within before handing them over. "It seems that you are finally managing to deliver work to the standard I expect."

Ben flicked through the pages to find a red '1' circled at the end of each piece. Inside, he gave a whoop of joy. He knew damn well that any other professor would have been grading his work with top marks for the last two years, but this was the first time ever that Professor Ellis had done so.

"Thank you, sir. This means a lot." Ben risked a smile.

"Don't get complacent." The professor paused for dramatic effect. "Now, you completed your dissertation over the summer, didn't you?"

Ben nodded. It had been a few months of hell getting it completed but his course demanded that it be submitted at the start of the third year.

"It's been through the grading panel. Would you like to know your result?"

Ben swallowed. The grade for his dissertation would likely determine the final grade for his degree, it was such a large proportion of the mark. He hadn't expected to get the news so soon, though. Usually dissertation grades were dished out just before

Christmas so that students could go home and either celebrate or mourn their performance.

"I suppose I should find out," he said hesitantly.

Professor Ellis raised an eyebrow. "Anyone would think I was about to stab you with a ceremonial dagger. Stop panicking. You got a first."

"No! Really?" Ben thought he might have misheard.

"I'm not in the habit of lying to my students, Mr. Astor. Congratulations. I wasn't on the panel but I read your work and the grade was well deserved." He sipped his tea. "Of course, the first has to be ratified by a viva."

Ben swallowed. A viva was a verbal exam designed to check that a given grade was deserved, or if a candidate was borderline between two grades it would decide which was the most appropriate. The idea of defending his dissertation verbally was terrifying.

"I thought we'd do it now." Ellis smiled as the shock registered on Ben's face.

Ben almost ran from the room.

"You can't! I need time to prepare…"

"You should know your subject well enough without preparation. I know you, Benedict, preparation time would get you tangled in knots."

"This must be against the rules…" Ben looked at the implacable face in front of him and realized that arguing was not going to get him anywhere. It briefly crossed his mind that Lucien might have taken lessons from this utter bastard.

"It is entirely within the rules and I have the full support of the faculty. Now, if you're finished complaining…" Ellis didn't wait for an answer, but launched into two hours of the most intensive questioning Ben had ever experienced. It was like being cross-examined as a hostile witness by a combination of Joe McCarthy and John Hathorne. By the time it was over, he felt as if he had been fed through a mangle. His head pounded and his muscles ached with tension.

The Professor handed him a fresh mug of tea and watched him with narrowed eyes. "The first stands. Well done."

Ben was too stressed to feel any elation at all. He still had his finals to deal with in six months' time—the dissertation had just been the first hurdle.

"Providing you maintain this standard, I would like you to work for me when you graduate, Mr. Astor."

Ben nearly choked on his drink. "Sir? I don't understand…"

"I thought we had just identified that you had a brain, boy. Please try to use it. I have three book commissions to complete in the next three years. I need an assistant. You would work toward your Master's and Doctorate at the same time."

Ben was amazed. Anton Ellis was a highly respected and successful academic author, sought after for lecture tours and media appearances. Working for him would be an apprenticeship that would guarantee entry into the inner circle of literary expertise in the country. It was an unbelievable opportunity.

"Today, the viva…?"

"Was an interview of sorts, yes. Your first was never in doubt. If you think I'm a bastard now, believe me, that opinion will not change if you decide to take up this job."

Ben could well imagine. But the pain would be worth it, he knew.

"I'm really flattered, sir. Thank you. I need to take everything in. When do you need an answer?"

One dark eyebrow rose slightly. "How long do you think you'll need?" His tone implied that any time would be a concession.

"I just need to talk to…" Ben hesitated. He wasn't sure whether to admit to needing someone else's approval for a decision that should be his alone.

"You want to discuss this with Lucien Thorne? I thought that might be the case." Professor Ellis smiled knowingly. "Fine. I'll see you tomorrow at four."

"You know…?"

"I know Lord Thorne very well, Benedict. I know that the two of you are together and I also know that he would expect you to talk to him about this, though I can assure you that our connection has nothing to do with this offer."

Ben stood to leave, feeling as though the whole world knew more about his relationship than he did.

Professor Ellis handed him a printed sheet. "Stop gaping, boy. It's very unattractive. Here are your assignments for the next week. Now stop taking up space and get out. Go and talk to Lucien. Ask him about me if you must. I'm sure his insights will be enlightening."

"He didn't give me the bruises, sir." Ben felt the need to ensure that there was no doubt about his injuries.

"Oh, I know that. Lucien would never abuse your trust." It was a strange choice of words. Ellis shooed him from the room, a knowing smile twitching his lips.

More than a little dazed, Ben did as he had been told and wandered across campus to a small coffee bar in the student union building. He ordered a double espresso and sat in a quiet corner to look over his assignments so that he could get to the library and research the books he would need. He wondered how he managed to be drawn to such dominant men.

Professor Ellis had the same aura of command that Lucien did. Ben found him attractive, though not in the same physical way as Lucien. *Bossy, the pair of them. But they both make me feel safe. They both care about me even if it's hidden behind an assertive, macho front.* He chuckled, getting a few glances from other patrons of the coffee bar. *What would Lucien say if he knew I was comparing him to my professor!* The light on his phone was flashing and there were three messages waiting for him, all from Lucien. His stomach knotted as he opened the first message, half expecting to be dumped by text.

Stop analyzing, idiot.

Despite the words, that made Ben feel one hundred percent better, if a little worried about how well Lucien knew him and the way his mind worked. He opened the second.

Trust me, beautiful.

Ben's face heated. He took a hasty glance around to see if anyone had noticed. The third message was a little more cryptic.

A or B?

He sighed, and punched in a response.

What am I choosing between?

To his surprise a reply came instantly.

Are you questioning me?

Yes.

Ben felt safe in his reply, knowing that Lucien was miles away at work.

Brave boy. Just something to improve your focus when rowing. Now choose.

Ben looked at the screen on his phone and wondered exactly how Lucien managed to be so dominant via text message.

A.

As he pressed send he wondered what he was getting himself into, but this time there was no reply. He looked at his watch. He had a few minutes to get some books from the library before his last lecture.

Chapter Fourteen

Ben cycled home along the river, warmed by an inner glow. He hadn't arranged to meet Lucien until the following morning, but he had a feeling he wouldn't have to wait that long and he was right. Lucien's Aston was in the otherwise empty car park. Lucien was leaning against it, dressed in an immaculate dark suit, his hair only slightly ruffled by the light breeze. Ben's stomach flipped over and his dick jerked happily. Lucien looked hot in rowing gear. He was drop-dead gorgeous in a tailored suit. He was typing rapidly into a BlackBerry, but looked up as Ben cycled toward him. The smile in his eyes betrayed him, even if it didn't reach his lips.

"Grab some kit—we're going to the gym." He bent his head back to whatever he was doing.

Ben took five minutes to get his kit bag and by the time he had returned to the car, Lucien was waiting in the driving seat.

"We need to do some time tests so I know how close you are to being good enough."

The car pulled smoothly away as Ben buckled his seatbelt.

"Good enough for what?"

"To race with me in the end of season meeting against Thamesmead."

Ben looked at him curiously. "Is it that important? It's just a friendly season closer."

"Not this year. There's a little more at stake."

What the hell was he talking about? Slowly, realization began to dawn and Ben turned to him. "What have you done Lucien?"

"Saved the club, I hope. Though that depends on you."

"This is to do with Seb, isn't it?"

"I've made an agreement with the club captain at Thamesmead. If we beat them in the double sculls race in two weeks' time, they will return the deeds to the boathouse. If we lose, Okeanos is no more, the club will be dissolved and the members absorbed into Thamesmead. They at least have a sense of fair play and want to keep the deeds through rowing effort, rather than Seb's stupidity."

Ben swallowed. "So why don't you just bring in someone else? Someone better than me, for fuck's sake."

"One of the conditions. I have to row and the pairing has to be with a current club member. There is no one better than you at Okeanos at the moment."

"Just wonderful. I'd be flattered if this wasn't so terrifying." Ben closed his eyes and massaged his temples. "Does Seb know about this?"

"Yes. In fact, he's meeting us at the gym tonight to help out. He may be a stupid prat, but he's a good coach when he puts his mind to it, and nobody else at the club is going to know about this. Another condition.

Nobody in the wider club will know the stakes we are competing for."

"How come Seb's not in jail?"

"I'm his mother's lawyer. He's out on bail. He'll probably end up with community service in the end. Up until now, his record's clean and he didn't actually get away with anything."

Ben didn't know what to say to that so he spent the remainder of the journey wondering how he could ever be good enough to win the race. Lucien made him work hard when they rowed, but Ben knew that he had always held back. Lucien was in another league entirely.

When they arrived at the university gym, there were only a few spaces occupied in the car park. That didn't mean much, not that many students could afford cars, but the gym was open to the public on a pay-as-you-go basis as well. Ben followed Lucien inside and the gym did prove to be quiet. They signed in at the desk and skirted the side of the machine room to get to the men's changing facility. Seb was already waiting for them next to the indoor rower. He didn't meet Ben's eyes, but set about calibrating the machine. Ben and Lucien went to change, and Ben was so distracted that he fumbled his way through the process. Lucien pressed against his back, slid a hand up Ben's top and pinched a vulnerable nipple.

"Ouch! Lucien, what the…?"

Ben swiveled around, extracting himself from Lucien's arms. "Oh! I didn't even notice you undressing."

"Had to get your attention somehow, you were off with the fairies."

Lucien wore nothing but a white cotton jockstrap. Ben's tongue all but lolled from his mouth.

Turn round, turn round, turn round… Ben's prayer was silent but ardent—he desperately wanted a look at the back view.

Lucien smirked, turned to the bench where his clothes were piled and bent over.

There is a God! "Oh, fuck!" Ben nearly came there and then. Perspiration broke out on his forehead and his groin ached.

Lucien pulled on his shorts and T-shirt, then turned and sat on the bench to lace his running shoes. He didn't look up, but amusement was apparent in his voice. "Perhaps now you'll be excited enough to row faster."

Refusing to rise to the taunt, Ben left him and wandered back to the machine room. He went straight over to the indoor rower. Seb stepped away from the ergo so Ben got settled in the seat. He pushed his feet into the straps, took up the handle and pulled back until the wire connected to the flywheel resisted. He let it go and made a couple of adjustments to the seat position, ensuring that his back wouldn't be under too much strain, then took up the handle again.

"It's calibrated for Olympic training. See what you can do," Seb said. He stood back and watched as Ben pulled on the wire, testing the resistance.

Lucien joined them and climbed onto a treadmill positioned directly opposite Ben. Ben warmed up slowly, gradually increasing his effort until he was going flat out. The seat slid easily on its track, letting Ben focus on driving his legs, taking and releasing the strain. He could feel the burn in all his major muscle groups. His breathing rate increased and sweat slicked his skin. His jaw tensed and he grimaced. He sucked in a huge lungful of air, gasping with effort. *How the hell long do I have to keep going?* He didn't have the energy to ask the question, but it kept repeating itself in his head. Just when he thought he'd have to give up, through the pounding in his ears, Ben heard Seb speak.

"You can slow down and stop now."

"Oh thank God!" Ben slowed far too fast but his arms had turned to overcooked spaghetti and he had to take a break.

Lucien was jogging slowly on the treadmill, watching with a particularly annoying grin quirking his lips. Ben scowled at him and bent forwards to hug his knees. He was close to throwing up.

"Okay, that was a decent warm-up," Seb said. "Now we'll do a timed session. Twenty minutes as fast and hard as you can manage."

"We? Where's the 'we' here, Seb? I don't see you killing yourself."

Seb played with the digital controls while Ben glared first at him, then at Lucien.

"I'm helping you, aren't I? Believe me, there are several thousand things I'd rather be doing right now, including sticking knitting needles in my eyes."

"Be nice, Seb, or I'll make sure to suggest to the judge that your community service should take place with the water board's sewer cleaning team," Lucien said as he upped the pace of his run.

"What about him? When does *he* get to be tortured?" Ben waved weakly in Lucien's direction.

Seb snorted. "He trained earlier today and is as good as ever. It's your lazy arse we have to worry about."

"Seb…"

The warning note in Lucien's voice was enough to generate a grudging apology, but Seb soon got his revenge. At the end of the twenty minute timed session, Ben was a sweating mess, his chest heaving as he dragged in fresh air. He didn't even have the energy to swear.

"Hmm. Not bad, I suppose," Seb said, looking at his stopwatch. "Could be better. Still, we've got two weeks to get you up to speed. Now go and run on the treadmill for twenty minutes, then we'll do this again. And, Ben, I mean run, not stroll, jog or fucking pansy around, okay?"

"Fuck off, Seb." Only pride gave Ben the will to walk to the treadmill. He'd much rather have rolled off the ergo and crawled.

Lucien chuckled and kept running. "It'll get easier, I promise."

"Right," Ben said with a healthy amount of skepticism. "So says the ex-Olympian who's been training like this for years."

Two hours later, Ben could hardly walk and Seb was tutting over his performance figures.

"I'll need you here every day, twice a day until the meeting or we won't stand a chance."

"We? This is all your fucking fault, Seb! What's your contribution to this fiasco going to be, apart from pissing me off?" Ben lay flat on his back on the machine room floor.

Seb looked like he was going to explode from the frustration of not being able to shout back, but Lucien was watching. "I'm going to do your job at the boathouse while you train." He turned on his heel and headed for the locker room.

Ben rolled onto his stomach, dragged himself up to his knees then hauled his body upright. He sat on the edge of the weight bench and put his head in his hands. "I must have been evil in a previous life. Vlad the Impaler, probably. Or Caligula, maybe."

Lucien massaged the back of his neck. "You realize that Caligula was known for his sexual adventures before he became truly psychotic, don't you? And anyway, I've got the monopoly on evil, remember?"

"I said previous life, not now!"

"Time we were going home, I think. You clearly need a little reminder of the dynamic in this relationship, Benedict."

Ben met Lucien's gaze and winced.

Chapter Fifteen

It took Ben a few minutes to realize that they were heading out of town, toward Lucien's home, rather than back to the boathouse after they left the gym.

"I don't have any overnight things with me, Lucien. Can't we go back to my place first?"

"For what I have in mind you won't be needing clothes. I have a spare toothbrush you can use. Seb will be opening the boathouse in the morning, so you don't need to worry about getting back early."

Ben flushed and fidgeted in his seat. He didn't have a counterargument worth using.

"And besides, I can deal with you better at my place."

"What exactly do you mean?"

"Ben, you've been pushing me all day. Questioning, challenging... I warned you what would happen if you didn't behave appropriately."

Ben wanted to disappear into his seat. Lucien's tone was so calm and controlled, it was scary but such a turn-on.

"I know a place that serves food until ten. We'll stop for something to eat on the way. That will give you a little more time to consider how you are going to apologize and make it up to me."

"Apologize for what, exactly?" Ben was exhausted and couldn't help but sound a little petulant.

"More attitude? Really?"

Ben looked at him in disbelief, but Lucien's face was totally implacable. They stopped at a quaint country pub. Lucien rejected the restaurant in favor of a quiet corner in the bar. He ordered grilled chicken salad for both of them, and it came with the most amazing homemade granary bread. Ben found that he did have an appetite, despite the butterflies in his stomach and wolfed down the food like a starving man.

"You'll need to watch your diet over the next couple of weeks," Lucien said. "Regular meals and more protein than you would normally eat. We'll save the carb loading to the week before the race. You're going to be burning a huge amount of calories."

Ben chewed and nodded dutifully. It was hard to think about rowing when his head was full of all the things Lucien might do to him that night. He would have liked to lose some of his inhibitions through alcohol, but Lucien bought him an orange juice without asking what he wanted.

"No drinking until after the race. Then I might allow you a celebratory pint."

"We have to win first."

"Yes, we do and it's not going to be easy. Thamesmead have a strong pair and they've been rowing together for a long time."

Ben pushed his plate away. "This is impossible. I'm going to let you down. Let everyone down."

"Not a chance. You're forgetting what an obstinate, stubborn arse I am. I don't like to lose, Ben, and I'll do everything I can to make sure you're ready."

"You dumped all this on me today, and still..." Ben bowed his head and tried to stop tears prickling behind his eyes.

Lucien gave him a hard look and didn't answer until they were heading back to the car.

"Your punishment tonight has nothing to do with the race. One text—that's all it took. One word in fact."

Ben groaned. "You asked if I was questioning you."

"And you typed yes. I haven't forgotten the spanking you earned on the river this morning either."

Despite his fatigue, Ben's cock perked up. Ben clenched his fists, frustrated that he had no control over his body's reaction to Lucien's words. *There really is no hope for me. He's bewitched me somehow. I should be running for the hills and yet all I crave is Lucien's touch, however harsh it might be.*

* * * *

Despite the unfairness of it all, Ben followed Lucien meekly into his bedroom. From the moment Lucien had indicated that punishment would be administered, his cock had been misbehaving and he was achingly hard, his balls tingling in anticipation of what would come.

"Take your fucking clothes off." Lucien stood with his back to the bed, hands clasped behind him. "Do it slowly."

After showering at the gym, Ben had donned an old T-shirt and sweats. Removing the garments was not the sexiest process. Ben did his best, baring his top half before removing his trainers and socks, then wiggling out of his soft trousers. His underwear was black, plain and functional. If he'd known he was going to be performing a striptease, he might have packed something a little more revealing. He hooked his thumbs under the elasticated waistband and rolled his shorts down before kicking them away.

There was something so erotic about being naked while Lucien remained fully dressed. That feeling of total vulnerability sent thrills through Ben's body and his face heated at the thought of how his cock was jutting proudly forwards, the head gleaming and wet.

"Very nice. Put your hands behind your head."

Ben laced his fingers together and did as Lucien ordered. The position left him even more open to scrutiny, and Lucien stalked around him, examining every part of his body. Ben shivered. He watched, wide-eyed, as Lucien went to his wardrobe and pulled a large chest from inside. He lifted the lid and examined the contents.

Ben wondered exactly how many toys Lucien had in his toy box and whom he had used them on before. His nervous anticipation grew when Lucien produced a set of heavy leather restraints.

"Keep your hands where they are."

Lucien buckled thick straps around Ben's thighs. Each strap had two loose ends.

"Lower your arms." The second straps locked Ben's wrists to his thighs. The thigh restraints were tight enough that he couldn't slide them down his legs, and it was incredibly frustrating that his hands were so close to his cock, yet he couldn't touch it.

"Legs apart."

Ben shuffled his feet farther apart, taking care to keep his balance.

Lucien circled him slowly, trailing a finger across his still bruised arse before dropping to his knees and taking Ben's full, slick length into his mouth. Ben jerked in shock. Lucien applied warm, wet suction and began to rhythmically squeeze his balls.

"Keep fucking still."

Ben froze. He didn't want to do anything that might cause Lucien to stop. If this was punishment, Ben resolved to misbehave more often.

Lucien licked with gently tormenting flicks of his tongue and began to push his finger between Ben's arse cheeks, which were tensed to hardness.

Ben wanted to scream. He was so close to coming, but just as he thought he would explode, Lucien withdrew and moved away. Ben thought he might cry, it was so cruel.

"On the bed. Now."

Bound as he was, Ben had to shuffle across to the bed, drop back onto the mattress then use his feet to push himself up the bed.

Lucien leaned over him and stroked his hair. "Do you feel sorry yet, Ben?"

He showed Ben a bottle of oil, poured a liberal amount into his hands and rubbed them together.

"Make a sound and I gag you."

He slicked the oil across Ben's chest and took each nipple between thumb and forefinger. Slowly at first, then harder, he rolled and pinched repeatedly until a whimper escaped Ben's parted lips.

"Oh, dear." Lucien didn't sound upset at all. "I did warn you."

The gag was leather, with a rubber piece that filled Ben's mouth and compressed his tongue as Lucien buckled the thing around his head.

"As you can't speak, or gesture, we need an alternative safeword. I'm going to put a bell ball into your hand. If you need to safeword, drop the ball."

Ben clenched his fingers around the small globe of plastic that Lucien pressed against his palm.

He rolled and squirmed as much as the bondage allowed him to, but there was no escape. Cool oil dribbled down the length of his cock and too-gentle hands rubbed more oil into his balls, never pushing enough to allow him to come. The tortuous massage continued for a lifetime, or so it felt to Ben, hovering so perilously close to the edge. When Lucien finally stopped Ben couldn't differentiate between the relief and panic that coursed through him.

Lucien grabbed some tissues and cleaned the oil from his hands. Ben then watched with rapt attention as Lucien slowly undressed and stroked himself a little before rolling on a condom. He shoved a couple of pillows under Ben's back, then climbed onto the bed. Kneeling between Ben's legs, pushing them even farther apart, Lucien leaned forward and kissed him over the gag, biting down on his lip. He then trailed his tongue the length of Ben's body, the wetness interspersed with small nips and light kisses. Then suddenly, Ben's legs were over Lucien's shoulders and Lucien was using more oil to slick Ben's hole. He could feel Lucien's cock probing gently at his entrance and he cried out into the gag.

With a jerk of his hips, Lucien entered him in one deep, penetrating movement. He paused, stroking his fingers across Ben's taut stomach muscles before withdrawing completely and thrusting again. Ben screamed into the gag, agony and ecstasy building to unbearable levels as Lucien repeated the movement again and again, stopping each time to stroke and touch but never going near Ben's cock. With his hands strapped to his thighs, Ben could only suffer the torment and use his eyes to plead for mercy.

Lucien watched the expressions flicker across Ben's face and hesitated. For a moment Ben thought he might relent and give him what he needed, but that was too much to hope for. Instead, Lucien began to grind slowly in and out, hoisting Ben's legs higher, bending him back to gain deeper access. Ben swore and moaned into the gag, desperate for release. Lucien slowed his thrusts even further and gave him an evil smile. "Are you sorry, Ben? Do you promise to be good from now on?"

Ben nodded frantically. Muffled sounds of begging came from his mouth and Lucien laughed. Grasping Ben's hips, he began to speed up his movements, slamming into him with punishing intensity. At the exact moment that Ben thought he couldn't take any more, Lucien wrapped a hand around Ben's cock and rubbed his thumb across the sensitive head. It was enough. They came together, hard and fast, Lucien shouting Ben's name in triumph.

Lucien moved Ben's legs gently down to the bed and withdrew from him as he softened. He used a finger to draw patterns in the creamy globs that spattered Ben's stomach and chest before releasing the gag.

"Fucking bastard!" Ben yanked on his restraints. The bell ball in his hand jingled.

"That doesn't sound like contrition, Benedict." Lucien thrust two fingers into his arse and twisted. "And I thought you loved me?"

"Stop! Stop…please! I'm sorry. I do love you."

"Better. Now, you just lie there like a good boy, while I clean up."

Lucien took his time, leaving Ben slumped over the pillows, still restrained, covered in cum, helpless.

When he returned, naked and smelling of soap, he held the chastity device he had used before in his hand.

"No!"

Ben's protests were futile as his flaccid dick was locked up, this time with a padlock and key.

"You can shower with it on." Lucien released Ben from his bondage. "Hopefully this will teach you to behave a little better in future, and if you wake me up appropriately I may release you in the morning."

Ben bit back a retort and glared at him.

"Oh, and I thought you might like to see choice A?"

Ben turned to see what Lucien was holding in his hand.

"This should make rowing tomorrow morning a very stimulating experience, don't you agree?"

Ben's eyes widened. The black plug was huge.

"Even more so after I've delivered that spanking I owe you."

Chapter Sixteen

Ben swallowed and felt his arse clench as he took in the ribbed, silicone plug nestling in Lucien's hand.

He shook his head slowly. "You are not putting that bloody thing in me."

Lucien gave a feral smile. "I'm not asking you, Benedict. Tomorrow morning, your beautiful arse is going to get acquainted with my little friend here. If you can row at top speed with this inside you, I'll know that you have the focus needed for us to win the race in two weeks' time."

"It won't fit."

"Yes, it will."

"How about I just promise to concentrate?"

"What are you worried about, Ben? It's not as big as me. It won't hurt. You might even enjoy it."

"That's hardly the point." Ben's voice trembled slightly. His swollen dick disagreed entirely with his resistance. Lucien wouldn't force him, but if he issued an order Ben knew he'd cave in.

"Nobody will know."

"You will."

Lucien grinned. "There is that. However, this is not a debate. Why don't you take a shower and consider the fact that even though I hold the key to you ever getting off again, you still insist on resisting me."

Ben had been so distracted by the thought of the large, bulbous plug being shoved unceremoniously up his arse that he had forgotten about the acrylic prison housing his dick. He clenched his teeth and bit back the sarcastic comment that he really wanted to spit in Lucien's direction and stalked to the bathroom.

Ben turned the shower up to the highest temperature he could deal with. He stood beneath the spray and let the heat soothe his abused muscles. The events of the day, the stresses and strains on his mind and body, were catching up with him, and Lucien's penchant for sex toys was the least of his worries. After a couple of minutes, Lucien came into the bathroom and joined him in the shower.

"I thought you got clean already?"

"You can never be too clean." Lucien pumped gel into his hands and smoothed it into Ben's skin. "And besides, I thought you might like the company."

Ben leaned back, pressing his back to Lucien's chest. "I'm so tired."

"You worked hard today. I'm proud of you."

Ben hummed his pleasure as Lucien massaged lather into his tight shoulders.

"I really wanted to hit Seb."

"I'd rather you didn't think about that idiot while we're naked together."

Lucien slid his hands down Ben's back, then dug his thumbs into Ben's glutes.

"Oh God, that feels so good. I've strained muscles I didn't even know I had."

"It *will* get better, I promise."

Ben appreciated the encouragement even if he didn't entirely believe Lucien.

"I heard today that I got a first for my dissertation."

Lucien spun him around and cupped his face. "You did? That's amazing. How come you waited until now to tell me?"

Ben rolled his eyes. "I had a few other things on my mind."

Lucien kissed him, with so much gentle tenderness that tears welled in Ben's eyes.

"We'll have a proper celebration when all this rowing business is over and done with. Champagne and strawberries. Naked. In bed."

That sounds perfect." Ben yawned. "Sorry."

"You can tell me all about it tomorrow. Now, I need to get you tucked up in bed before you fall asleep right here."

"Mmm, 'kay." Ben let Lucien guide him from the shower, then stood passively as Lucien dried him with a big, fluffy towel. Tucked between the cool sheets, under Lucien's luxurious duvet, Ben couldn't recall the short walk from the bathroom. He was aware of Lucien's warmth and strength wrapped around him and the last thing he felt as he drifted off, was a soft kiss on his cheek.

* * * *

The next day the river was serene and calm, the weather still and cool. None of those adjectives could be applied to the way Ben felt as every pull on the oars drove the plug in his arse against his prostate. He took a few deep, cleansing breaths and ignored the demands of his over-stimulated body. He was hyper aware of Lucien in the seat behind him, probably grinning at

Ben's predicament. At least he wasn't suffering the torment of chastity as well, though it had been a close thing.

The alarm had gone off early enough that it had still been dark. Lucien had work commitments and they'd needed to be on the river by first light, at around six. Reluctant to leave the warmth of the bed, Ben had disappeared beneath the covers and had taken some of his own frustration out on Lucien's stiff morning erection. It had been deeply satisfying to hear Lucien's muffled curses as Ben had willingly rolled his lover's balls around his tongue and had mouthed them gently. In the dark, Ben had used his hands, lips and tongue to bring Lucien to the edge of orgasm before taking him deep into his throat, constricting the tip of his dick just as he had come. Ben had had to swallow three times, then had licked up the sticky remains coating the head of Lucien's cock. That had brought more swearing and Lucien dragging him above the covers for a deep, demanding kiss.

Desperate to have his own aching dick released, Ben had hoped in vain as Lucien had retrieved the plug from the bedside cabinet and had peremptorily ordered him to roll over. Cold lube had slicked his hole and had coated the device, which had slid into his accepting channel with little resistance after an initial push. He'd hated to admit it, but Christ, it'd felt good. Not as good as Lucien filling him completely, but good. The look on his face must have given him away, because Lucien had started playing with the plastic sheath and voicing his concerns about just how uncomfortable it must have been at that moment.

He'd been right. Every movement had seemed to push the plug deeper and Ben had felt his cock fighting to harden. The flexible spikes had dug into his length and he'd squirmed, only causing himself more problems. Lucien had made him wait until the very last minute before removing the bloody thing.

And now here he was, attempting to maintain his dignity and row like a professional whilst a fucking piece of silicone played havoc with his sanity.

He was tempted to roll the boat just enough that Lucien would fall in.

"You're smirking, aren't you?"

"Possibly. Wouldn't you if our positions were reversed?"

Ben gave that a moment's consideration. He couldn't imagine ever being as dominant as Lucien.

"I hate you."

"I know."

They didn't have enough breath for long sentences, but some conversation was a nice distraction from the relentless pace.

"So why do I love you so much?"

"I'm irresistible."

"You're irredeemable."

"That too."

"Everything hurts."

"Good."

"Charming!"

"Pain means you are trying hard enough."

The lactic acid burning in all his major muscles didn't seem to be an appropriate reward for the amount of effort Ben was putting in. He stopped talking, blanked his mind, ignored his rock-hard dick and the continuous burn of pleasure in his arse and rowed.

They went a little farther than normal and Lucien guided the boat toward the shore, pausing at a sheltered spot overhung with a canopy of weeping willows. Instead of turning the boat to head back,

Lucien unstrapped his feet and stood before carefully jumping into the shallows and heaving the boat aground.

He stretched out on the bank and waited for Ben to flop down next to him. A thick carpet of moss covered the ground. The lush dark green was highlighted by golden spots in places where the sun broke through the shifting umbrella of leaves. It was a bit damp, but the coolness against Ben's heated body was welcome. Lucien rolled onto one side, propped himself on an elbow and gave Ben a calculating glance.

"Take your shorts off."

"What? No! Someone could see!" Ben peered toward the water but the willow's trailing branches touched the ground, protecting them almost entirely from view.

"Ben, we're in the middle of nowhere. The only thing likely to ogle your arse is a passing duck."

He snarled as Ben edged away from him. Before he could get too far, Lucien was kneeling over him, laughing as Ben giggled and squirmed. Lucien yanked Ben's tight shorts down and pulled off his tented jockstrap. Roughly, he pushed Ben over and wiggled the plug in his arse before gently extracting it. A couple of hard slaps followed.

"When I tell you to do something, Benedict, fucking do it!"

Ben snorted. He rolled onto his back and gave Lucien a scathing look, still struggling beneath his spread, muscular thighs. Then he dissolved into another fit of the giggles.

"I can't believe you're doing this!"

Lucien wrapped a hand around Ben's cock and squeezed. "I was going to treat you to a little relief, but I don't think you deserve it. You're lucky I haven't got any condoms with me or I'd give your arse a good pounding for this attitude."

He moved up Ben's body and rested his weight across his middle, pinning him down. Lucien rolled the top of his own shorts down and a raging hard-on sprang out. Ben squirmed and struggled, trying not to lick his lips, but soon Lucien was pinning his shoulders and thrusting his dick down Ben's throat.

Ben didn't really have a chance to do anything himself. Lucien was totally in control, just giving him time to breathe before filling his mouth again and again. He came quickly and Ben swallowed gratefully, pleased that he had managed not to gag. Then Lucien wrapped a warm hand around his cock once more, and slid it rapidly. Ben pulled his knees up, unable to hold on as Lucien jerked him faster and faster.

"Holy fuck!" He came hard into Lucien's hand, grass and twigs tangling in his hair as his head slammed back onto the bank.

"There, you see? I can be kind and giving." Lucien wiped his sticky fingers on a large dock leaf before relaxing back onto the grass. He pulled Ben over, letting him nestle into the curve of his neck.

"Can I please put my shorts back on?"

"No. I think you look better in just the top."

Ben pulled his knees up, trying to hide himself, but Lucien shoved them back down. "Lie still. I want to be able to look at you."

Being naked from the waist down, out in the open, was not something Ben was comfortable with, however isolated the spot. Lucien rested his hand gently on his stomach, stroking him lightly, which sent quivers through Ben's body.

"Relax. Enjoy the moment."

"Dear God, Lucien, what are you trying to do to me?"

"I just like to touch you. You have beautiful skin."

"There you go. Just as I start to believe you're the devil incarnate, you go and say something like that!"

Reluctantly Lucien removed his hand. "I suppose we should be starting back."

"Please tell me you're not going to make me row back half naked."

"I'd be tempted, if it were just us. But no. I've told you before. Your body is for my eyes only. You can get dressed."

Heaving a sigh of relief that Lucien hadn't reinserted the plug, Ben pulled on his underwear and shorts. The water felt cool on his bare feet as they paddled out to the boat and got in. Ben's muscles, still pleasantly warm, relaxed into a steady rhythm, and on the way back he and Lucien concentrated on synchronizing perfectly rather than on raw power.

As they took the boat back to the racks, Ben was sure people were giggling and looking in his direction. Lucien had an annoying smirk on his face as well.

"What is it? Do I have a smudge on my face or something?"

"Not quite." Lucien began to pull bits of grass and leaves from Ben's hair.

"Oh, my God!" Ben's face felt like it was on fire and he fled up the stairs to his flat.

Lucien followed at a more leisurely pace. "What's the matter? Are you embarrassed that everyone knows I had my wicked way with you?"

Ben yanked open the fridge door and let the cool air wash over him. He grabbed two bottles of water and threw one at Lucien. "Yes! I won't be able to look any of them in the eye ever again!"

He slumped in a chair and ignored Lucien's smug smile. "As far as I'm concerned, the more they understand that you are mine, the better."

Ben just groaned miserably.

Lucien grinned. "I'll take a quick shower, then I need to go."

"Wait! I completely forgot to tell you... I had a job offer yesterday." Ben sat up a bit straighter. "Professor Ellis wants me to work for him after I graduate. I have to give him an answer this afternoon and I wanted to ask you what you thought."

Lucien didn't look in the least surprised.

Ben held the cold water bottle to his forehead before removing the cap and taking a deep swallow. "You knew? Ellis did say you and he were acquainted, but..."

"I've known Anton for a long time," Lucien said. "He was a friend of my father's. He was around quite a bit while I was growing up." His tone implied that there was a lot more to it than that. "He did ring to let me know he was going to ask you. Did you enjoy the viva, by the way?"

"He told you about that too? It's a fucking conspiracy."

"Not at all. He was informing not asking, and the decision is yours, Ben. The job offer had absolutely nothing to do with me. It's your future, your choice."

"So you wouldn't mind?"

"No, I wouldn't mind. Quite the opposite. I think it would be an amazing opportunity if you can put up with the bastard."

"I put up with you..." Ben hid a smile.

"Ben, you really have to learn a little more respect." Lucien's voice was deadly quiet. "I don't have time to deal with you now, though I should bend you over my knee. I'll pick you up from the gym this evening. Seb's expecting you at six. You'll need to go in at lunchtime as well—he's going to leave instructions for you."

He disappeared into the bathroom, leaving Ben to wonder if deliberately provoking Lucien was such a good idea. The thrill of anticipation told him that it was.

As he was leaving, Lucien kissed him uncharacteristically softly—another warning. "Oh, I forgot something too—Maddy wants you to come to the filming at the weekend. I'm brat-sitting on Saturday afternoon so you can help me with pest control then stay over and take a look at the chaos on Sunday. A break from training will do you good. *Rowing* training, that is."

With that parting shot, he was gone.

Chapter Seventeen

At seven-thirty that evening, Ben waited outside the gym, a small overnight bag at his feet. Seb had left earlier to do lock-up duty at the boathouse, and it was a good job he had or Ben thought he might have been tempted to kill him. If it wasn't for the race... Still, even after one day of proper training his times had improved slightly. That was only minor compensation for having to put up with Seb's pushy, arrogant nonsense. He was a lot braver when Lucien wasn't there to keep an eye on him, but as Ben no longer had to worry about job security he made sure that Seb knew he was no pushover. Ben was very happy to be submissive for Lucien and it was in his nature to want to please others, but in Seb's case, Ben discovered an inner dominant streak that rose to the surface with every rude remark.

Lucien pulled into the car park a few minutes later. Ben was leaning against a wall, his hair lifting in the breeze. He knew he looked tired — it was in his posture and the dark circles beneath his eyes, which he'd noticed in the locker room mirror when he was drying his hair. He hoped that Lucien's plans for the night included a little TLC, for once. He gave a small smile as Lucien executed a handbrake turn and the car settled in a cloud of dust.

He picked up his bag and walked around to the passenger side of the car. He opened it and leaned in.

"You're such a show off."

Lucien quirked an eyebrow. His eyes sparkled with mischief. "Get in, Ben."

Ben settled in to the passenger seat of the Aston and relaxed. The low growl of the car's engine was soporific and he fought the urge to close his eyes and sleep.

"So, was Seb a complete bastard?" Lucien put the car into gear and pulled away without any dramatics.

"You need to ask?"

"Do you want me to have words with him?" Lucien patted Ben's thigh.

"No. What he says makes sense — it's just the way he says it. I can deal with him, don't worry. I have to learn to stand up to him. After what he did to me, he should think himself lucky I'm not pressing charges for assault."

"What were your times like today?"

"Slightly better. I still wanted to throw up after the timed session."

"A minor improvement each day is what you should aim for. Push too hard and you'll end up injuring yourself."

"Seb knows when to stop, I'll give him that."

Lucien grunted. "Well, just let me know if I need to slap him around a little."

"You'd enjoy that wouldn't you?"

"Damn right."

Ben giggled. He was tired enough to feel a little lightheaded.

"How did it go with Ellis?" Lucien asked. "You were seeing him this afternoon weren't you?"

"He was pleased I said yes, I think. It's hard to tell with him. He acted like he hadn't expected anything else and then gave me extra assignments. He did bring out the chocolate biscuits, though, and that doesn't happen often."

Lucien chuckled. "That sounds about right. Anton expects to get his own way."

Ben turned to look at him. "He was more to you than just your father's friend, wasn't he?"

For a moment Lucien didn't reply. "Let's just say he taught me a lot and leave it at that."

"He's straight, though—married?"

"Now he is. He wasn't always, though. I don't really want to talk about it."

Lucien clammed up and refused to say anything else.

Ben closed his eyes. He had no intention of pushing Lucien for information he didn't want to share. His past was his business. He had to admit it was intriguing. If Professor Ellis and Lucien had been involved in any kind of relationship, there must have been fireworks involved. Not those pretty, sparkly ones either—loud, explosive, light up the sky ones.

* * * *

By the time they'd parked at the main house and made the walk to Lucien's place, Ben was flagging. He could barely keep his eyes open. Sleepwalking took on an entirely new meaning. Lucien threw together a quick pasta dish with a rich tomato sauce and crusty garlic bread.

"I don't think we need to worry about either of us having garlic breath tonight," Lucien said.

Ben shoveled his food down like a starving man. "Wow, this is good."

"You really are hungry, aren't you?"

"I'm hungry all the time at the moment." Ben chomped on another piece of bread.

"Lots of exercise will do that. You need to eat more than you've been used to. I don't want you keeling over during a training session."

Ben murmured agreement but kept eating. The food revived him a little but by ten o'clock Lucien seemed to see that he had had enough.

"Come on, let's put you to bed." He slung an arm around Ben's waist and propelled him toward the stairs.

"I'm sorry, Lucien, but with academic work and all this extra training..."

"It's all right, there's no need to apologize. I'm asking a lot of you. You need to rest and I can spend more time plotting how to punish you appropriately."

Ben gave him a sleepy but indignant glare.

"I wish I had the energy to tell you what I think of that, but I don't." Ben undressed and slid beneath the covers before Lucien could change his mind and decide to tie him somewhere inconvenient and not conducive to sleep. To his surprise and delight, Lucien stripped off and climbed in next to him. He wrapped Ben up in a comforting hug. It felt so good. Ben found himself moving so he could press his face against Lucien's chest and throw one arm across his waist. The last thing he knew before he slept was the rise and fall of Lucien breathing beneath him and a gentle hand stroking his hair.

* * * *

Ben awoke to something hard prodding lightly at his arse, and he shifted further onto his side to grant Lucien better access. Lucien stroked Ben's bare shoulder then slipped his hand across his chest to tweak a nipple. Heat flooded Ben's body. He squirmed, wanting more.

"How long have you been awake? It's not even light yet."

"Long enough to know that one night off is all you are going to get. I was so horny last night it hurt." Lucien's breath was minty fresh. He'd managed to sneak out of bed and return without Ben noticing.

"You didn't fuck me in my sleep, then?"

Lucien snickered. "I prefer to hear you begging for mercy."

The he proceeded to ensure that Ben did just that. He'd already prepared himself with a condom and a nice coating of lube, making Ben wonder how deeply asleep he had been to miss all the action.

Lucien curled an arm over Ben's hip and stroked his dick.

"Seems like you're ready for me."

Ben could only manage an incoherent squeak.

"Curl your knees up to your chest."

Still on his side, Ben balled himself up and yelped as Lucien slid two fingers into him with no warning. The initial slight burn soon faded to a pleasurable throb.

"Mmm. So good."

"I need in." Lucien's voice was rough with desire. He withdrew his fingers, and Ben whimpered at the loss.

"Need you too. Please, Lucien."

Lucien thrust into him at an angle that pressed all the right buttons. Ben pushed himself back, taking Lucien's length as deeply as he could. Lucien slung a long leg across his hips and squeezed his thighs together.

"That feels...so fucking tight!" He thrust his hips back and forwards half a dozen times as Ben moaned and whimpered.

"Harder! I need more..." Ben pleaded.

"Demanding this morning, aren't we?" Lucien flipped Ben over onto his knees and covered him with his body. Grabbing Ben's narrow hips, he moved faster, harder. Ben urged him on, frantically pulling on his own cock until he came with a cry, shoving back until he was so deeply impaled he could no longer move. Lucien threw his head back and screamed his own release before they collapsed in a hot, sweaty heap.

For a while the only sound was heavy breathing. Lucien flopped onto his back.

"Don't move. I'll deal with the condom and fetch a towel." He half rolled, half fell out of bed.

Ben had no intention of moving ever again. He lay sprawled in a boneless heap, a sappy grin pasted on his face. He hadn't moved an inch when Lucien came back and gave him a gentle clean up.

"You look utterly gorgeous. I wish I could keep you like this always, well-fucked and in my bed."

Ben rolled onto his back and held out his arms. "Hug."

When Lucien smiled, Ben's insides melted into goo. Lucien clambered into bed and pulled Ben onto his chest. He yanked the covers over them, and Ben snuggled shamelessly against him. Post-sex cuddling was the best thing ever. Lucien stroked his arse. Ben kissed the curve of Lucien's neck.

"It would be nice, wouldn't it?"

"What would?"

"To hole up here for a few days and enjoy each other."

"I wish we could." There was a hint of longing in Lucien's voice.

"But it's impossible. I know. I didn't mean to make you feel bad." Ben clung to Lucien.

"You didn't, love. We can make plans for Christmas. It will give us something to look forward to. You, me, lots of toys from Santa."

"Does Santa deliver the kind of toys I think you're suggesting? Wouldn't that put you on the naughty list?"

"There's naughty and then there's *naughty*." Lucien couldn't have sounded more lascivious if he tried. "Santa fully appreciates the latter, I'm sure."

"It's all kinds of wrong that you just suggested Father Christmas is into kinky sex." Ben shook with a fit of the giggles and received a slap that warmed his backside nicely.

"Quiet, brat, we can fit another half hour's snooze in before we have to get up."

"Half an hour, huh?" Ben could think of a lot more fun things that could be achieved in half an hour. He wiggled, rubbing his cock against Lucien's.

Lucien stretched out an arm and groped around the bedside table. He handed Ben a shiny foil packet.

"Climb on, sweetheart. Hands behind your back. I want to see if you can come untouched." His grin was devilish.

Ben pouted but his cock stiffened. "Fine." Lucien's eyes narrowed. Ben ran his tongue over his lower lip. "Fine... Sir."

* * * *

As it was Friday, it was a routine day. After rowing, Lucien disappeared to his usual round of legal meetings and estate business. Ben fitted two more gym sessions in around lectures and library time. They rowed again in the evening but kept the pace steady. The river glittered silver in the rising moonlight as they left the boat for Seb to put away before heading upstairs to pack Ben's things for the weekend.

"Was I imagining things, or did Seb actually look happy this evening?" Ben shouted from the bathroom as he took a quick shower.

"His mother's kicked him out and his girlfriend's dumped him. He's sleeping on a mate's couch, though from what I hear he'll be moving into the bedroom pretty soon." Lucien replied.

Ben thought he might have water in his ears. "No way! Really? No wonder he looked less grumpy. Perhaps he'll be less of a bastard at the gym next week?" He slung a towel around his hips, then poked his head around the bathroom door.

"Not likely. I've told him to keep pushing you." Lucien's blue eyes were calculating as he took in Ben's expression. "Whatever you are intending to say, don't. Your arse is already overdue a good spanking and I need to conserve my energy for the race."

"Unbelievable." Ben pulled on old jeans and a light sweater. He started to pack for two nights away.

"You respond better to a hard taskmaster."

That statement had all kinds of hidden connotations and Ben knew better than to respond. Arguing with Lucien was a waste of breath and he already looked stubbornly attached to his point of view.

"It's reading week next week, isn't it?" Lucien asked.

"Yes. I really need to catch up on some preparation or Professor Ellis will have my hide. He's treating me like an employee already and I don't think he recognizes employment law. He's still somewhere in the Middle Ages in that regard."

"You'll stay with me next week, then. You can pick up fresh clothes when we row and borrow one of the estate cars. It's too far to cycle to the library when you are training as well."

"Okay. Thanks."

Lucien raised a dark eyebrow. "What, no argument?"

"I'm not giving you any more ammunition than you already have, my love. I value my ability to sit down." What Ben didn't say was that he was secretly pleased to be asked.

"Hmm, I have been threatening a spanking for a while now. I should really deliver on my promises and you have been getting a bit bratty recently."

"Don't feel obliged," Ben said, backing away slowly. His rapidly hardening cock pressed against resistant denim.

Lucien chuckled. "Don't panic. You'll keep for later."

"You're evil. You know that, don't you?"

"Finish packing, Ben. It's my turn in the shower." Lucien stripped naked right there, dropping his clothes where he stood.

His erection bobbed enticingly, and Ben licked his lips. He would happily drop to his knees if Lucien asked him. All those perfectly sculpted muscles were worthy of worship but Lucien strolled straight past him.

Ben wanted to whine his disappointment. Instead he threw a few more things into his holdall and zipped it up, muttering curses under his breath. He didn't care if Lucien heard him. If it added a few more strokes to the impending spanking, Ben would be content.

* * * *

At home later that evening, Lucien cooked and produced a remarkably good chili, not so hot that it destroyed all sense of taste, but with a nice after-burn. A cold beer would have been good to wash it down with, but they both sipped mineral water and stuck to the 'no alcohol' agreement. Lucien had some case notes to prepare and worked for an hour while Ben cleaned up the kitchen. It was all very domestic and settled. Every now and again, Ben caught Lucien looking at him as he pottered around, trying to be quiet so as not to disturb him. Those looks made him blush, and when it was finally time to go to bed his pulse was fluttering wildly.

Lucien pushed his chair back.

"Come here." When he could reach Ben's hands he pulled him over to stand between his knees. "You make the most tedious work bearable." He moved his hands from their resting place on Ben's hips to his arse. "It's excellent motivation to get finished when I know you are waiting for me."

Ben suddenly felt very shy. He pressed his teeth into his lower lip and looked down. "Does this mean I'm forgiven?"

Lucien sank his fingers into Ben's buttocks, holding him in place. "Don't be ridiculous. Forgiveness is no fun at all. Now take off your top."

Ben's lower lip trembled just a little.

"Fuck, you look absolutely adorable when you're nervous. I need a picture of you with just that expression, all big shiny eyes and pouty lips. Delicious."

Ben scowled. He pulled his T-shirt off over his head and threw it onto the couch. He looked down into Lucien's blue eyes, which showed his intent. Ben tried to twist away but Lucien just pinned him tighter.

"There's no escape, Ben. You want this as much as I do."

Ben could feel a rising ache in his nipples and prayed that Lucien would know what he craved. He wasn't disappointed as Lucien flicked each throbbing bud hard enough to sting before trailing his fingers the length of Ben's torso to his waistband.

"These needs to come off. Now."

Ben kicked off his trainers. He wore no socks so didn't have to struggle awkwardly to get rid of them. He did have to wiggle his hips to get his jeans down past Lucien's restraining thighs. His pure white shorts hugged every contour of his body, and Lucien murmured his satisfaction before stroking the ridges and valleys that twitched beneath his exploration.

"Tell me what happens when you are disrespectful, Benedict." Lucien's voice sent delightful chills through Ben's entire frame.

"You punish me." His cock jerked as Lucien flicked at it through fabric damp with pre-cum.

"As is my right." Lucien held Ben's eyes, challenging him to respond.

Ben had to force the words out, "Yes, sir."

"Very well. Remove your underwear and lie across my knees."

Ben took a pace back and tried not to panic. This was a big step and he just hoped he was ready for it. He found it hard to understand why he was so hard. His cock clearly didn't recognize humiliation — or if it did, it wasn't bothered. At all. His heart pounded. Lucien just gazed at him calmly, waiting for him to obey. Why did he have to be so fucking handsome? Ben couldn't resist those eyes or the curve of Lucien's soft lips.

Terrified but exhilarated, Ben pushed his shorts down and kicked them away. Prostrating himself across

Lucien's muscular thighs was the hardest thing he had ever done. Every atom, every molecule of his body screamed 'run'. His wretched cock had entirely different ideas, however. Thankfully, his hair flopped forwards to cover the burn on his cheeks and the tears welling in his eyes. How must he look with his arse in the air, submitting voluntarily to Lucien's commands?

Lucien stroked Ben's back and the curve of his arse. He edged forward just a little, adjusting his position so that Ben's cock was lodged between Lucien's thighs. Lucien dragged a finger between clenching cheeks.

"So beautiful."

Ben jerked beneath his touch.

"And responsive." Lucien made him wait a little longer as if allowing him to experience the feeling of total helplessness before bringing one hand down across his backside with a resounding *thwack*. Ben's skin burned, on both sets of cheeks. He got even hotter when Lucien said softly, "Count for me, Benedict."

"Two!" Ben gasped the word as he was soundly spanked for the second time.

"No, no. Start from the beginning."

Ben counted from one to ten. By the end he was squirming across Lucien's lap, desperate to get away from the pain, even more desperate for another blow.

"If you don't keep fucking still, I'll give you ten more." Lucien stroked his glowing skin softly, licked his finger and speared Ben's hole with it, twisting and turning it slowly.

Ben screamed and came hard, the results of his ejaculation splattering the floor, mixing with his tears.

Lucien removed his finger and patted Ben's arse gently.

"Stand up. Hands behind your back and look at me."

Legs trembling, face streaked with wetness, Ben did as he had been told.

"Go into the bedroom, beautiful. In the bottom drawer of the chest you will find a collection of toys. Choose two. Place them on the bed and then wait for me. Kneeling please, Benedict."

In the bedroom, Ben rubbed a hand surreptitiously across his eyes and took a deep breath. His tears had resulted from an overdose of emotion rather than pain. His arse did hurt, but he was already at half-mast again. He wanted to check out the marks in the mirror but didn't dare. He knelt at the drawer and pulled it open not knowing what to expect.

"Oh, God." Some of the things inside he didn't even recognize. His hand wavered over crops and paddles, chains and straps before he picked out a simple pair of handcuffs. In one corner of the drawer was a stack of underwear in various fabrics. He pulled out a pair of boxer briefs in some kind of wet-look rubber. The back was open and the front had an interesting vertical zip. Ben smiled to himself and wondered if he dared.

He laid both items on the bed and dropped to his knees, facing the door. He put his most angelic, innocent look on his face and waited. A few minutes later, just long enough for Ben's knees to start aching, Lucien strolled in and walked over to the bed.

"Intriguing choices. I wouldn't normally allow you clothing, but these are…interesting." He held up the skimpy, scandalously revealing shorts.

Ben ducked his head to hide his smile. "I didn't choose them for me, Lucien."

Lucien froze and grabbed a handful of hair, pulling Ben's head back. "That spanking taught you nothing, did it?" He sounded angry but there was humor in his eyes. "What am I going to do with you?"

"Put those on and fuck my brains out, hopefully." Ben whispered the words under his breath but knew Lucien would hear.

"If I wear these for you, then I choose the other toy. The instruction was two, after all."

Ben was torn. He desperately wanted to see Lucien in those shorts and was amazed he was even contemplating putting them on, but Lucien would no doubt choose something awful and there had been a lot of gleaming metal in that drawer. His arse was also very sore and the thought of those paddles and crops was enough to make him wince. Still, it would be worth it.

He nodded assent, but doubted that his agreement had been needed.

"I have something I was saving for later, but I think you deserve it now."

That didn't sound good. Ben shifted nervously on his knees and debated whether or not to try appealing to Lucien's forgiving side. He decided it was pointless. The man *had* no forgiving side and Ben had taken himself down this path—he had to see what was at the end.

"Get on to the bed and sit against the headboard. I don't want you going anywhere."

Lucien used the handcuffs to attach one of Ben's wrists to the wooden rail, then disappeared downstairs. When he returned he was carrying an icebox, which he put down at the side of the bed before slowly stripping off his clothes in a way that sent Ben's temperature soaring.

If Ben had thought that Lucien would be self-conscious about wearing the shorts he had chosen, he couldn't have been more wrong. Lucien looked as confident as always and there was no sign of redness on his perfect face. Ben knew that if he had been made to wear them he would have been the color of a ripe tomato from head to toe. Lucien acted as if they were completely normal attire, even though the zip at the front was being severely tested. He turned around and bent over to pick up his discarded clothes, and Ben moaned. The sight of a perfect bare arse, tightly framed by the clingy black rubber, was almost enough to make him come.

Lucien turned back and smiled knowingly. "You're looking a little flushed, Benedict. Perhaps you need cooling down?"

He released Ben from the bed rail and cuffed his hands together instead. "Lie down and turn over."

With his hands cuffed in front of him, it was more comfortable to lie with them stretched above his head, but this meant that Ben couldn't see what Lucien was doing.

"Lift your hips." When Ben did, Lucien shoved a cold, rolled-up towel beneath him, raising his arse in the air.

"Lucien, what exactly are you doing?" Ben was starting to feel a little nervous.

"Cooling you down." He rummaged in the icebox and took out a U-shaped piece of metal, slightly shorter on one side than the other. One end was tipped by a flat metal loop, the other by a shiny sphere of solid metal. He sat on the bed next to Ben's head and turned it over in his hands. "You see, this end"—he fingered the loop—"fits against the small of your back so that a belt can be passed through to hold it in place."

He paused, waiting for Ben to realize where he was going with this. Ben looked anxiously at the size of the silver ball glinting in the lamplight.

"You can probably guess where the other end goes. It's also been in the freezer." He squeezed a small amount of clear lube onto the ball and spread it around with the tip of his finger. "Wouldn't want to warm this up too much... Just enough that it doesn't burn you. Where this is going a cold burn would be most unpleasant."

"Lucien..."

Lucien unzipped the front of his shorts, allowing his cock to spring free. "What?"

The objection that Ben had been about to utter slipped from his mind as he was mesmerized by the sight in front of his eyes. Then Lucien knelt across him and pushed the ice-cold metal ball into his channel.

How could something so cold feel as if it were on fire? It felt... He couldn't describe how it felt. It was amazingly good, but as Lucien slipped a narrow belt through the ring against his back and ordered him to turn over, it also felt humiliating. He was rock hard again, turned on by sensation and the sight of Lucien kneeling across him, his cock jutting from those shorts, but he almost felt like crying. Why did he allow Lucien to do these things to him? There was no question that he had allowed it—Lucien had used no force, no persuasion. It was as if just the tone of his voice and a look from those beautiful eyes were enough to take any resistance out of Ben's reach.

As Lucien fastened the belt buckle around Ben's waist and leaned back to admire his handiwork, Ben caught him off balance and reversed their positions. Lucien looked surprised, but for Ben it felt exciting to be taking some initiative. Knowing what was held inside him, feeling the ball press and move, made his cock twitch with excitement.

Ben shuffled backwards and slid onto his front so that he could take Lucien into his mouth without needing his hands for balance. The warmth of pulsing flesh in his mouth contrasted with the ice-cold throb in his arse. Desperate for Lucien to touch him, Ben distracted himself by plunging downwards, taking Lucien deep into his mouth and sucking hard. He could exert some control this way and it made him feel stronger.

Lucien twitched under his ministrations but made no sound until his body gave up any resistance and he came with a hot gush into Ben's throat. Licking his lips, Ben took a calculated risk and maneuvered himself so that his own cock was above Lucien's face. He still waited for permission. When Lucien nodded Ben grasped the bed rail and pushed his dick past Lucien's lips to the warmth within. He moved gently, tentatively, not sure how hard he could thrust, but Lucien grasped his hips and pulled him deeper.

It was all Ben could do to hold the rail and keep still as Lucien sucked, licked and bit lightly. Lucien held his hips tightly and Ben knew that his lover was still completely in control. Then Lucien slapped his sore arse and the ball inside him pushed against his prostate. Ben screamed. His cock pulsed and streams of cum flooded Lucien's mouth. Then the world disappeared.

* * * *

"Ben, are you all right?" Lucien slapped his face gently. "You blacked out."

It could only have been seconds. Ben moaned. The fucking ball was still inside him. He felt giddy and exhausted. He was lying on his side, so he must have collapsed on top of Lucien and been rolled over, but he didn't remember anything after a moment of intense, blinding pleasure.

"You're going to kill me."

Lucien chuckled and stroked his hair before releasing the handcuffs and undoing the belt around Ben's waist. "Push out gently."

The ball slid easily free and Lucien got up to fetch a cool washcloth from the bathroom. He returned, minus the shorts, and slipped back into bed. Gently he wiped Ben's face and neck, then his stomach and around his softening dick. Ben giggled. "That tickles."

"Are you feeling better?"

"I was feeling pretty bloody good before. I don't know what happened."

"It doesn't matter. As long as you're all right. I didn't push you too hard?"

Ben snuggled into Lucien's hard body and wondered at the uncertainty in his voice, something he had never heard before.

"Ben? You would tell me, wouldn't you?"

"Yes. I'd tell you. I have a safeword and I know how to use it." Ben was fading fast into sleep. "I love you…"

Chapter Eighteen

By seven the next morning, Ben and Lucien were up to their ears in dung, cleaning out the stables. It was barely light and a hard frost made the warmth inside very inviting. Huffs of horse breath steamed into the air, and Ben fancied that his equine friends were quietly chortling to themselves. Two humans committing hard labor in their care was, apparently, highly amusing.

Once they were done shoveling and Ben had snuck carrots to all the horses, they did a quick change into running shoes in the tack room. Lucien took the lead on a cross-country run that had Ben believing he was overdue a coronary. Misty rain soaked their clothes and hair until the weak autumn sunshine fought back and broke through the cloud layer. Mud-like glue sucked at their feet and spattered their legs. At the point Ben thought he could just lie face down in the mud and end his suffering, Lucien stopped. He bent double, hands on his knees, taking deep breaths. Then he sat on a nearby tree stump and steamed almost as much as the horses had.

Ben wheezed and panted. "It's good to know that you can get tired too."

"Sit down. I want to talk to you." Lucien patted the trunk next to him.

Ben gave him a curious glance but did as he'd been asked.

"Last night, I was serious when I asked if I'd pushed you too far, Ben. I love you and I don't want to hurt you. Ever." Lucien sighed. "I know I can be...a bit...well, you know."

"Arrogant? Demanding? Professional bastard?" Ben watched as Lucien's eyes narrowed.

"Mmm. Yes, I suppose so."

Ben smiled at his grudging admission. "Lucien, I'm with you because I want to be. Please credit me with a mind of my own."

"I just..."

"I love you for asking and I promise I will tell you if there's ever anything I don't want to do, okay?"

Lucien kissed him softly, tenderly and Ben felt a warm glow inside.

"Of course, nothing I could ever do to you will compare with this afternoon," Lucien stated grimly.

"How can you, of all people, be scared of two six-year-old boys?"

"Freddie and Jason. Brilliant names. Maddy swears it's a coincidence but they would make great horror film characters. Those two are demons in disguise. Perfect little angels at home, but as soon as they are out of sight...! I took them to the zoo once. I've never seen lions look scared before."

Ben kissed him on the cheek. "Don't worry, I'll protect you. We'd better go, hadn't we? We need to build in some resuscitation time because the return journey is going to kill me before the kids get a chance."

They ran back home for a quick shower and change before heading up to the main house to collect the boys. Maddy was waiting in the yard when they got there. The twins were hiding behind their mother, each clutching one of her hands.

Maddy gave Lucien a kiss, then hugged Ben. "Hey, gorgeous. I hope little brother is treating you well?"

"He has his moments." Ben caught Lucien's glare and pressed his lips together with a grin.

"Well, he had better be. Thanks for taking the boys this afternoon. The film crew are doing a really expensive scene today and the boys are driving them potty."

Lucien growled, dropped to his haunches and suddenly the boys were climbing all over him with delighted cries of, "Uncle Thorny, Uncle Thorny!"

"Thorny?" Ben chuckled as his lover became a human climbing frame.

"When they were smaller they couldn't pronounce Lucien and I wasn't going to put up with Lu. This seemed appropriate." Lucien hoisted one boy under his arm and headed for the door, while the other decided that Ben would make a good climbing frame too. Maddy gave him a pitying look as they headed for the car.

"Family dinner tonight—don't forget. That's if you both survive of course. I packed a bag with spare clothes, picnic, snacks, drinks, wipes, soft toys, cattle prods. You know, the usual kit."

"We'll be back in plenty of time." Lucien handed over a small bag. "Can you look after this? It's a change of clothes for tonight. It will save us going back to the cottage."

They used Maddy's car and Lucien took great delight in strapping the boys into the back. "Excellent. Now they can't move for twenty minutes."

They might have been immobile but they definitely weren't quiet. Choruses of, "Where are we going?" became increasingly shrill until Lucien gave in.

"To the adventure playground, you little rug rats. That should wear you out." He turned to Ben. "It's a circuit training track around the lake, which means you get to have a go too."

Screams of excitement from the back indicated approval. Then there was much frantic waving as Lucien pulled away and Maddy receded into the distance.

* * * *

They stopped for a picnic lunch, in a field next to the river. Ben was amazed at how much food two young boys could firstly consume and secondly plaster all over themselves. He and Lucien took one each and went through half a packet of wipes removing sticky patches and various unidentified substances. They locked up the car, then spent three hours tackling every obstacle on the circuit three or four times. The boys absolutely loved it, clambering fearlessly around and swinging from ropes and bars like monkeys. What they loved best was watching Ben do pull-ups or climbing ropes while Lucien counted or made sarcastic comments about how slow he was. The course ran alongside the water but the boys were good about not getting close to the edge, they were too busy trying to outdo each other.

They bought enormous ice creams, Lucien insisting that flakes were mandatory. He'd had the foresight to stuff the remaining wipes in his pocket so was able to give the boys a post-ice-cream scrub down. Ben saved his cone and they all fed bits of wafer to the ducks before heading back to the car, exhausted. Within five minutes of being strapped into their seats, the twins were asleep.

"Maddy's going to kill me because they won't sleep later. Sweet revenge!" Lucien said as he got behind the wheel.

"It was a great afternoon. I watched you with them. They love you to bits and you are brilliant with them."

"Just don't tell their mother."

Ben smiled to himself. Maddy wasn't daft — she would already know.

"I think they adopted you into the family as well, Uncle Ben." Lucien pulled away and turned toward home.

"You torturing me was great entertainment for them."

"It could have been worse. I could have sent you to the gym with Seb."

"God no! I've had more than enough of him in the last few days. This was a much better workout. In fact, I think I'm going to follow the boys' example and nap on the way home." He closed his eyes and reclined the seat a little.

"Great. Relegated to chauffeur again."

Ben snuck a peak at Lucien. He was smiling.

* * * *

Back at the house, Maddy threw the two filthy children into the bath while Lucien introduced Ben to her husband, James, over mugs of tea. They clicked instantly. James was broad-shouldered and softly spoken. In his mid-thirties, he was a little older than Maddy and clearly doted on her and the boys. With the twins fed and put — protesting — to bed, Ben and Lucien took turns in the bathroom and changed out of their mud-spattered clothes.

They settled down for a grown-up dinner in the very grand formal dining room.

"Why are we eating in here, Maddy? It's a three-mile hike from the kitchen," Lucien asked.

"Because it's Ben's first family dinner with us and I wanted it to be special." She'd used all the fine china and crystal and there were fresh flowers on the table. Slender, tapered candles burned in ornate silver candlesticks.

"So James and I are not worthy of special treatment?"

Maddy looked from her brother to her husband. "No."

Ben loved it. The setting was magnificent. Maddy teased Lucien constantly and resisted her obvious urge to ask Ben loads of personal questions. James talked estate business with Lucien until the two of them received warning looks from Maddy, and over dessert and coffee the conversation turned to rowing and the big race.

"I still can't believe you did it, Lucien. What were you thinking?" Maddy scolded.

"They wouldn't give house room to anything else. We're lucky we have this opportunity to get the deeds back at all."

"But poor Ben didn't get any choice." She patted Ben's hand.

"Poor Ben is a big boy, Maddy. He could have refused."

Not strictly true, but Ben wasn't going to argue.

"He's too nice for you to abuse. What if he gets fed up of you?" She gave a sidelong glance at Ben.

"A little abuse never hurt anyone and Ben's not going anywhere." There was just a hint of threat in Lucien's voice.

Ben didn't know where to look. He settled on James who gave him a sympathetic shrug.

Maddy grinned impishly. "Carry these plates to the kitchen for me, Ben?"

He followed her on the long trek to the kitchen and put the stack of dirty dishes next to the sink. A pile of dogs around the Aga shifted. Heads were raised but apparently Ben and Maddy were not interesting enough for them to leave the warm spot.

"Is this your subtle way of getting me alone, Maddy?" Ben started to rinse the dishes.

"You don't have to do that, Ben. I'll get James to load the dishwasher later. And yes, it is." She beamed. "You're not fed up of him, are you, Ben? It would destroy him if you left."

Ben leaned against the sink.

"He's right, Maddy. I'm not going anywhere. I love him." The words were simple but full of certainty.

"I shouldn't even ask, but he's talked about you for so long and you are the first man he's ever brought here."

That was a surprise.

"Our father did not approve of Lucien's sexuality. No one wanted the rift to widen so Lucien never had boyfriends — didn't even consider it until after father died."

Ben had to stop himself gaping.

"I don't mean he's never been with men, obviously, but he's never committed. After he came out — he was eighteen — I think there may have been something

190

going on with a friend of the family, but if there was they kept it well hidden. Then Lucien went off to university and law school. There were casual flings, but nothing serious. Every minute of his spare time was taken up with rowing anyway. After the Olympics I think he realized that he had to dedicate some time to himself, so he retired from the elite level. He's twenty-five, Ben. He needs a proper, loving relationship. It took him a long time to decide to approach you — it was a huge risk for him."

Ben gave her a hug. "Lucien is the best thing that ever happened to me, Maddy. While he was watching me, I had a huge crush on him. I won't let him down."

"He can be..."

"It's all right. I know exactly how he is and I wouldn't want him any other way."

"Okay, then. Let's take a fresh pot of coffee into the lounge and I'll tell you all about this film-making malarkey."

She spooned coffee into an enormous pot, added water from a kettle standing on the Aga then loaded it onto a tray. Ben took it and followed her.

"This place is a maze. I'm sure I'd get lost if I was on my own," Ben said.

"You'll get used to it. You need to spend more time here rather than holed up in the cottage with Lucien." She gave him a mischievous glance, and Ben's face heated.

They trooped through the dining room, sweeping up James, Lucien and their coffee cups as they went. A door at the far end of the room led to a cozy snug where they settled around the fire. Maddy distributed drinks and handed round a box of mints.

Ben sat a respectable distance from Lucien on the couch, but Lucien growled and pulled him closer, putting his arm around Ben's shoulders.

"I promised to tell Ben about the film people," Maddy said as she sat down.

"Pain in the arse," James said. "But they bring in enough money to keep up with the maintenance of this place."

"How many weeks a year do you have people here?" Ben asked. "It must be very intrusive."

"Last year we had bookings for eleven months out of twelve, but one of those was for a big period film and they were here on and off for six months. The current mob are here until late November, then we have a break through to Christmas."

"And they're filming a new production of *Great Expectations*?" Ben asked.

"Yes. The director, Anthony Everson, is an American with a couple of Oscar nominations under his belt already. He's used the house before for some outdoor scenes in another film and he remembered us." Maddy smiled. "He's a nice guy. Tries to be as accommodating as possible and keeps his crew under control."

"That's because he's met Lucien." James snorted.

Ben glanced at his lover.

"What?" Lucien was all innocence. "I just laid down a few guidelines for him."

Ben could just imagine how that would have come across.

"He went all Lord of the Manor on him. Frightened poor Anthony half to death." Maddy took another mint. "Takes these away from me, James, before I go through the whole box."

When James leaned forward to do just that Maddy snatched the box away from him. He sighed heavily. Ben giggled and leaned against Lucien.

"Time we were going," Lucien said. "Once these two start fighting over chocolates, things tend to get nasty. Thanks for a lovely dinner, Maddy."

"Yes, I've had a wonderful evening." Ben stood and leaned down to give Maddy a kiss.

"I'll see you bright and early. Leave Mr. Growly-Pants behind, I'll chaperone you."

Ben grabbed Lucien's hand and pulled him away before sibling warfare started up.

* * * *

It was getting late by the time they got back to Lucien's house, but the brisk walk in the chilly air had woken Ben up. "Would you like a hot drink?" Ben moved toward the kettle but was captured by Lucien's embrace.

"I think my family already loves you almost as much as I do."

Ben relaxed into Lucien's hold. "I like them too. I miss having family around."

"Why did your parents move to Spain?"

"When Dad retired and sold his plumbing business, they just decided it was time to enjoy themselves. Good weather, lots of golf..."

"How did you feel?"

"I was a late child. Bit of a shock, I think, so they were that much older. I just want them to be happy and once I'm working I'll be able to afford to visit more often."

"Do they know about me?"

Ben chuckled. "Of course. I mentioned you a few times before we got together."

"Really?"

"I confessed to a bit of a crush, and I was showing off. You know, aristocratic Olympian—you're the stuff of fairy tales, and my mum loves a good unrequited love story."

"As long as it has a happy ending."

"You should see the list of questions in Mum's last letter! She wants a picture of you too."

Lucien hugged him tighter. "Make sure you send one that shows my best side. Did Maddy warn you off when she spirited you away to the kitchen?"

"No! She's very protective of her baby brother. She was worried I wouldn't be able to put up with you."

He felt Lucien stiffen slightly. "Do you want me to change? Be...nicer?"

That made Ben laugh out loud. "I love you just the way you are. I don't want to change you— I want to keep the man I fell in love with."

"Thank God for that. Now get naked—I've been itching to get my hands on you all evening."

Chapter Nineteen

Ben was up early the next day, tiptoeing around as he dressed and had a quick breakfast. He went to say goodbye to Lucien who was buried beneath the duvet. Even in his semi-comatose state, Lucien managed to deliver a kiss and engage in a bit of groping before he let Ben go. Maddy was meeting him by the lake, where the film crew was setting up for an early morning scene where Pip meets secretly with Estella. Not strictly true to the book, but close enough. Ben was really excited — he couldn't wait to see how everything worked.

As he walked across estate land, there was a distinct nip in the air. The forecast was for an unseasonably cold day so Ben had dressed accordingly. He was wearing a heavy sweater over a long-sleeved T-shirt and jeans, thick socks and boots. A woolly hat covered his hair. When he reached the lake, Maddy was equally bundled up, one gloved hand wrapped around a large paper cup of steaming coffee. She held out a second cup to Ben.

"Morning, beautiful. How's the grouch this morning?"

"Still sleeping. The twins wore him out." He took the coffee. "Thanks for this, I didn't have time to make a drink at home."

She smiled. "The boys adore him. Lord knows why — he's so rude to them. I don't think I've ever heard him use their actual names."

Ben laughed. "It's a mutual appreciation society — he's just good hiding it. They're great kids."

She nodded. "Well, Sunday is Daddy's day. James keeps them busy with the animals and teaches them about the land. That's what he says he does anyway. He could be spending the day in the village teashop stuffing them with cake for all I know. I think they're both going to be natural farmers, though. They definitely have an affinity for all things muddy."

They walked across to where the film crew was bustling around, getting ready. A huge catering wagon was doling out breakfast and people wrapped in fleeces and scarves were sitting at plastic tables eating. The two principal actors were wearing long coats over their costumes to keep warm, but it still looked strange to see 'Estella', with her intricate period hairstyle, scoffing a bacon sandwich.

Maggie knew everyone and introduced Ben to people with all manner of interesting jobs. They were all very friendly and welcoming. When they got to the director, a surprisingly young guy with flaming red hair and a perpetually worried look on his face, Ben realized that Maddy must have already been talking about him.

"Maddy, my love, is this him?"

She nodded. "Yes, it is. Ben, this is Anthony Everson."

"Pleased to meet you." Ben was a little nervous and tongue-tied.

The handshake that followed was firm and warm. "I'm so glad you're here. I understand you can write? English major?"

"Umm, yes. I'm reading English." Ben looked at Maddy, who just smiled.

"Well, my fucking script editor has gone down with man flu and I need some line adjustments done. Maddy tells me that you're the perfect man for the job."

"She does?" Ben felt the stirrings of panic in his belly.

"She's been singing your praises." Anthony waved over an assistant. "Ben here is the new staff writer. Find him a pen."

"But I've never done anything like this before!"

Anthony's assistant thrust a biro and sheaf of papers into Ben's hand.

"Nor has anyone else the first time they do this. Most of the crew are barely literate unless you're talking tech production speak. They could be an alien species. So are you up for it?"

Ben swallowed. "Yes okay then, I'd love to help. Just don't expect miracles."

That was all it took. Maddy gave him a peck on the cheek and abandoned him with a parting comment to Anthony, "Don't you dare leave him alone with Taylor or my brother will string you up."

"Call me Ant, Ben. I hate Tony and Anthony is such a fucking mouthful." He put an arm round Ben's shoulders and walked him toward a tent. "So, you're with His Lordship, then?"

"Yes." Ben tried to take everything in as they walked.

"You must have nerves of steel and the patience of a saint, then — perfect for this job." He rolled his eyes and Ben laughed, feeling slightly guilty. "Lord Thorne is one scary individual."

"He isn't really." Ben felt the need to defend Lucien's character. "Okay he is… Until you get to know him."

"Well, he terrifies me. By the way, the Taylor Maddy was referring to is Taylor Sherman. He's playing the adult Pip. He's a promiscuous little shit who will hit on anything in trousers, but he's probably a future Oscar winner so I put up with him. You'll have to take him through any new lines, so just take anything he says with a pinch of salt."

They arrived at a spacious tent full of electronic equipment. There were a few tables and chairs and several computers.

"This luxurious accommodation is the production tent. You can commandeer a desk in here. The production assistant will relay the changes needed and you can mark up the paper script you're holding with your amendments. A runner will check them with me and then get them typed in to the electronic version. Does that make sense?"

"Sure. I'll just shout if panic sets in."

"No hyperventilating. This lot will just think you're an actor doing some weird breathing exercises or something. You could pass out on the ground and they wouldn't take a blind bit of notice."

Ant gave him a thorough briefing on what he needed that morning, and soon Ben found himself immersed in a frantic whirl of rewrites and revisions. The adaptation from the book was brilliant, but the practicalities of filming meant minor adjustments to dialog had to be made constantly. Ben enjoyed every moment and he had no idea what time it was when filming finally finished for the day. His stomach told him that lunch must be well overdue. He checked his phone and there was a text from Lucien.

"Picking you up for a late lunch. Great timing!" Ben said as he read the text. He stretched the kinks from his back and wandered out of the tent, stomach growling.

Ant waved then went back to an intense conversation with a cameraman. People hurried around shifting gear, packing boxes and preparing to move to a new location. Ben became aware of a presence at his shoulder.

"Oh, hello, Taylor." Ben felt doubly shy around the star of the show.

"Would you like to join me for something to eat?" Taylor asked. "I doubt Ant remembered to feed you."

Taylor Sherman was undeniably good-looking — the only problem was that he knew it. Ben had watched some of his scenes in between edits and he was an amazing actor. He was polite and friendly to the crew, coming across as self-effacing, but Ben had sensed that it was as much an act as the part he was playing.

"Sorry, I'm meeting someone. Thanks for the offer, though."

"That's a shame. You did a good job today. I was looking forward to getting to know you better." Taylor's green eyes glittered.

Ben could see Lucien walking toward them behind Taylor's back.

"Are you sure you wouldn't like to rearrange? There's a great little place I know." Taylor put a hand on Ben's shoulder and squeezed lightly.

Lucien had a face like thunder, and Ben had to hide his smile.

"I believe he said he was busy."

Taylor turned, startled.

"Can I introduce Lord Thorne, Taylor?" Ben said. "This is his estate."

Taylor held out a hand that was ignored as Lucien pulled Ben close and kissed him, long and hard. He finally pulled away and treated Taylor to his haughtiest stare.

"Go and get in the car, Benedict." Lucien's voice was a low growl.

Ben's dick jerked. He still didn't understand why he enjoyed being ordered around, but he did, especially when Lucien got all possessive.

"Yes, Sir," he said quietly, enjoying how Taylor's eyes widened. Taylor licked his lips. Ben headed for the car and left the two alpha males to face off.

As he climbed into the Aston, Ben felt almost sorry for Taylor. God only knew what Lucien was saying to him. Even from fifty yards away Ben could see that Taylor's complexion seemed to be a couple of shades lighter.

Lucien had a smug smile on his face as he stalked toward the car. The driver's door clicked open and Lucien slipped behind the wheel.

"He said you turned him down." Lucien rested his hands on the wheel. He tapped the polished wood in an agitated rhythm.

"Yes." Ben rested a hand on Lucien's thigh. "Of course I did."

"He's very good-looking."

"Lucien, don't." Ben tried to be patient. "You have to learn to trust me."

The words took Lucien's anger away instantly. "I'm sorry. It's a major character defect."

"Jesus, Lucien—did you just apologize?" Ben's jaw dropped.

Lucien scowled. "He won't be bothering you again."

"Thank you for taking care of me," Ben said without a trace of sarcasm. "I hope you didn't scare him too much. He didn't do anything wrong."

"He touched you."

"I'm sure he's learned his lesson." Ben gave Lucien's thigh a reassuring squeeze. "Now how about lunch. If you're going to act all caveman, you have to provide me with a stegosaurus steak now, don't you?"

That broke the tension. Lucien chuckled as he started the car. "Cheeky brat."

Ben tilted his head for a kiss.

"Demanding too."

Then he proceeded to steal Ben's breath away.

Chapter Twenty

The rest of the week passed in a blur for Ben, and he was sure it was no different for Lucien. They rowed twice a day, in foul conditions as the weather had taken a turn for the worse. Ben was at the gym twice a day as well, tolerating Seb as best he could. He helped out with script editing on the film set in between and kept up with his studies by working into the early hours. Lucien trained and worked tirelessly. Their relationship had to take second place for a while, and they were both too tired to do more than cuddle when they eventually collapsed into bed each night. Even Lucien's voracious sexual appetite had been dulled.

The race would take place on Sunday afternoon, the culmination of the otherwise friendly inter-club competition. Saturday, Lucien had decided, would be a rest day. There was no more preparation they could usefully do and they were both wound so tightly they needed to relax.

Saturday's chores were approached at a leisurely pace. The horses didn't complain and even the normally boisterous dogs lolled lazily in the stables. Of course, the rain was sheeting down outside. Ben inevitably lost the argument over who was going to wheel the barrow across the yard. As he went one way, miserable and dripping, the twins shot in the other direction at their usual unstoppable speed.

"Slow down, boys!" Maddy followed them more sedately.

Ben was on his return leg when he heard a child's shill scream from the stable. He dropped the barrow and tore inside, quickly taking in the scene. Maddy, distraught, clutching two howling boys. Lucien, white faced, sat on a hay bale with his fist clenched, blood oozing from between his fingers.

"Maddy, it's superficial. Just a shallow cut—it's fine."

"What happened?" Ben ran to kneel at Lucien's side and took his hand, prizing open the fingers.

"He just stopped Jason from jumping onto an open blade." Maddy was beginning to calm down. "Twine cutter, on the bales. He moved so quickly I couldn't stop him. Lucien grabbed the blade, pulled it away." She spoke in jerky, breathless sentences.

"I'm fine, don't fuss. Take the boys home," Lucien said, his voice strained.

"It's okay, Maddy, I'll look after him." Ben used his most reassuring tone.

Peace descended as Maddy and the boys finally left and Ben got a chance to look at Lucien's hand more closely. A long, shallow cut crossed his palm from side to side. It was messy—flecks of dirt and rust speckled the wound—but it wouldn't need stitches.

"Let's go home so I can clean and dress this." He didn't give voice to what they were both thinking—how the hell was Lucien going to row the next day?

Lucien didn't argue.

"I didn't think, Ben. All I could see was Jason's knee landing on the blade. I left it there... I'd been cutting open the bales for the hay bags."

"You weren't to know the boys were coming—they're not usually around on Saturday mornings. Don't blame yourself. You should be proud you prevented a nasty accident."

Ben pulled a clean handkerchief from his pocket and wrapped it around Lucien's hand, knotting it tightly.

"I'd never forgive myself if one of them got hurt."

"You're in shock. Both the boys are none the worse for wear. They're probably plaguing Maddy with gory tales of spurting blood and severed limbs by now."

Back at the house, Lucien didn't make a sound as Ben cleaned and dressed the wound. It must have been throbbing horribly and Lucien looked a bit shaky. It wasn't anything to do with the injury, but shock as what might have been played over and over in his head. Ben could almost hear the cogs whirring.

"Lucien, come and lie down." He took him into the bedroom. "Wait, let me cover the bed with towels. You're drenched." They'd walked back from the main house in a downpour. Ben fetched a couple of bath sheets and spread them over the bed, then he watched as Lucien sat back against plump pillows and made himself comfortable.

Lucien's eyes cleared. "I hope you've lured me here for a better reason than tea and sympathy, Ben." He crooked a finger. "Come here."

The order snapped across the room and Ben felt his cock jerk. He smiled, relieved that Lucien was back to normal.

"Benedict, I'm in pain. Can you imagine what that does to my normally patient, tolerant self?"

'Patient' and 'tolerant' were not words that Ben had ever thought to associate with the man he loved.

"Grouch."

"You did not just call me that."

"That's what Maddy calls you—I think I'm going to adopt it too."

"I still have one good hand, Ben. If you're not naked and over here in the next minute, it's going to be applied to your arse."

Ben had an instant flashback to the last time Lucien had had him over his knee and thought that it might be worth pushing a bit harder. Lucien's eyes glinted. "Don't defy me, Benedict. You *will* regret it."

Ben slowly began to pull off his damp clothes as Lucien watched, unblinking.

Ben pushed his sodden hair away from his face. Lucien gazed at him appraisingly. He felt brave and Lucien seemed to love the little bit of resistance, the hint of rebellion that underpinned Ben's submissive nature.

"You'll have to undress me. Buttons are difficult with one hand."

Ben had a feeling that Lucien was perfectly capable of using his injured hand, but said nothing. Still shy of his own nudity and the stiff erection he had no control over, he clambered onto the bed and knelt across Lucien's thighs. He had to part his own legs wide to do so, and it made him feel so vulnerable and exposed. What he really wanted to do was hide beneath the covers, but Lucien was watching with a knowing look on his face.

"You have a stunning body, Ben. Why are you so shy about it?"

"All very well for you to say, lying there fully dressed."

Lucien's gaze was focused firmly on Ben's cock. Ben's instinct was to cover himself, but before he could move Lucien reached out and wrapped his hand around his lover's pulsing member. Ben gasped as Lucien flicked the head before rolling his thumb around it.

"Let's see if you can tackle buttons while I'm doing this, shall we?"

Ben bent to his task and found that he was holding his breath. He really wanted to come, but Lucien was holding back just enough to prevent orgasm. He concentrated on exposing Lucien's broad, smooth chest and pushed his shirt off with a happy sigh before starting on Lucien's trousers. Lucien shifted his slim hips enough that the garment could be pulled down and off. A tight pair of shorts followed quickly, and Ben settled back into position and submitted to the agony of Lucien's hand on him. His nipples ached and he wetted his fingers before pinching himself gently. He rolled his head backwards and closed his eyes.

"Hey! Stop enjoying yourself and focus on me!" Lucien growled the words, but he was smiling. "You are going to fuck yourself on me until I come. I want to watch while you pleasure me but deny yourself release. Understand?"

He handed Ben a condom and raised an eyebrow when Ben hesitated.

"I've never been with anyone else, Lucien. I'd really like to feel you properly."

Lucien shivered. "I've never barebacked with anyone and I got tested before we slept together. But only if you're sure? It means so much that you trust me."

After flicking the shiny packet across the room, Ben grabbed the lube, coating Lucien's cock and cheekily massaging some around his smooth balls before reaching back to slick his own entrance. He positioned himself carefully and sank down slowly, trying not to wince as Lucien's thickness breached and filled him. He met Lucien's gaze and blushed as he started to rise and fall. It felt almost voyeuristic. Lucien watched his every move, smiling slightly, making no move to touch or help him. Ben's cock ached to be stroked and his hand drifted forward.

"Don't you dare. Come before I say you can and I'll keep you in that chastity device for a week."

Ben squeezed his inner muscles as hard as he could. The small gasp that escaped Lucien's lips was reward enough. Ben arched his spine and leaned back, supporting himself with one hand as he lifted and dropped with increasing speed. He could feel Lucien's heat within him and the world disappeared. There was just motion, friction, intense pleasure…

Lucien came with a hot gush and Ben stilled in an agony of frustration. His balls hurt, his cock burned and, when he opened his eyes, Lucien's smirk nearly pushed him into disobedience.

"Bastard! Please… I need to come."

Lucien pulled himself more upright, Ben still impaled on his lap. He began to play with Ben's hard nipples, rubbing gently, then tweaking and rolling before pinching harder and harder.

"Beg me. I want to hear you pleading."

"Aagh!" Ben squirmed from the delicious pain. "Please! Touch me… I'll do anything!"

"Anything?" Lucien's eyes narrowed.

"Yes! Anything you want… Just, please…"

Lucien applied his good hand to Ben's desperate cock while the other continued to torture his nipples.

"Come for me, Ben… I want to see."

Feeling the sweet pain of release, pleasure fracturing his vision, Ben spasmed into Lucien's welcoming hand until he was drained. He collapsed, exhausted, onto the covers.

"You see? That was worth a little patience, wasn't it?"

Ben raised his head, took in Lucien's smug expression and buried his face back in the pillow with a moan.

Chapter Twenty-One

They'd avoided any mention of how Lucien's hand was going to affect their chances the following day. As time had gone on, they'd both grown quiet and the tension in the air had been palpable. Their sleep had been disturbed, and by dawn they'd been too restless to stay in bed. A short run had cleared the cobwebs, and breakfast had gone some way toward settling Ben's queasy stomach.

Ben smiled wryly as they dressed in matching Okeanos kit. The dark green and black suited Lucien perfectly, and the clingy fabric formed to his muscles in a way that almost allowed Ben to forget the pressure they were under.

Lucien's hand was lightly bandaged, and he slipped a pair of gloves on to avoid the inevitable questions at the club.

Maddy, James, the boys and a few of the film crew were all coming to watch, so they set off in a small convoy and got to the river with the meet already in full flow. The spectators all headed off to find good viewing positions. Ben and Lucien made their way to the boathouse.

Seb was waiting for them and revealed that somehow, news about the deeds had leaked out. Everyone knew what was going to be riding on the last race of the day.

"Fuck." Lucien was not happy. "This was supposed to be kept secret."

"It wasn't me, Lucien, I promise." Seb looked miserable enough. If the secret was out then everyone knew what he had done, as well.

"Thamesmead, no doubt. Well, we'll just have to hope that it makes them look doubly stupid."

"I feel ill." Ben ran inside and made it to the bathroom in his flat just in time to throw up. Lucien followed close behind. He stroked Ben's hair while he lost what remained of his breakfast, then handed him a toothbrush.

"Just do your best, Ben. Whatever happens, that's what counts."

Ben splashed water on his face and gave his teeth a good scrub. The few paces from the bathroom to the couch might as well have been a mile.

Trembling, Ben sat on the edge of the sofa. "I don't want to let you down."

Lucien wrapped an arm around his shoulders. "You could never do that. I'm proud of you. You've worked so hard."

Ben glowed inside. Those few simple words meant so much.

"Ready to go?"

He'd never be ready, but, with Lucien there to support him, Ben nodded.

Outside, the cheers and shouts of the crowd were muted to Ben's ears by the pounding of his heartbeat.

They made their way down to the river and got comfortable on the scull while others held the boat still for them. They maneuvered the boat to the middle of the water and Ben glanced across at their opposition, immediately wishing he hadn't.

"Don't worry about them. Don't look at them. They may be in the Olympic squad, but that doesn't mean shit here," Lucien reassured him confidently.

Ben gave a slight nod and blanked out everything but his grip on the oars, the tension in his muscles and the unique bond between him and Lucien. He imagined silken strands joining their limbs to keep them perfectly synchronized. When the klaxon sounded, nothing mattered but their smooth passage through the water. Their breath steamed on the cold air and sweat coated their bodies as Lucien set a punishing pace. Ben was only vaguely aware of the other boat, how close they were. He could see people running and cycling along the bank in his peripheral vision, but if they were shouting and cheering he couldn't hear them. To him there was silence apart from the splash of water.

At the turn, Thamesmead were slightly ahead. Lucien's left oar handle was coated in blood, his knuckles white.

With five hundred meters to go, Ben heard, "Ready, now!" and they moved to an even faster stroke rate. Every muscle in his body screamed, and his heart was pounding. It seemed like hours rather than minutes, but then they were over the line—it was over. Bent double, Ben sucked in huge gulps of air.

"What happened? Did we win?" He could barely get the words out.

Lucien's laugh was slightly hysterical. "No idea!" He planted a kiss on Ben's neck. "You were incredible. Win or lose, that felt like a gold medal!"

Slowly the sound of shouting penetrated their exhaustion. Seb was jumping up and down on the bank like a lunatic. "You did it! You did it!"

Tears slipped down Ben's face. "Is it real? Did we win?"

"I guess we did." Lucien's laugh was a little hysterical.

Once they got to the bank and managed to disembark, there were hugs and kisses, slaps on the back, and the deeds were handed over with sporting grace.

"That was some of the best pairs rowing I've ever seen—and the bravest," Thamesmead's president admitted with a pointed look at Lucien's bloody hand. "If you ever fancy changing clubs…"

There was a splash behind them as Seb was chucked into the river. He managed to emerge with a shamefaced smile on his face and bits of green weed clinging to his hair.

"I deserved that."

It was all a bit overwhelming. The pressure of the race, the demands of the preparation, and suddenly it was over. Ben, for one, felt lightheaded with relief. A flute of champagne was thrust into his hand and he gulped it down like water. He clung to Lucien, needing his steady strength. Lucien answered questions, accepted congratulations and made small talk like a pro. Ben pressed to his side and focused on staying on his feet. After a while, Lucien made their excuses. They slipped away from the noise of the celebrations and headed home.

Chapter Twenty-Two

For Ben, the drive home passed in a blur. The single glass of champagne had left him with a pleasant drowsy buzz. He pressed his hot cheek against the cool glass of the window and closed his eyes. Lucien put on a classical station, and the soothing music lulled Ben into a doze.

Strangely, it was silence that woke him. He gradually became aware that the throb of the engine had ceased and the music had stopped.

"Hey there, sleepyhead." Lucien ruffled his hair. "You're back with me. That's good. I was considering reclining the seat and leaving you here to sleep."

Ben blinked a few times, clearing his misty vision.

"Are we home?"

"Yes. Well, we're parked at the main house. We still have to walk to the cottage."

"'Kay." Ben couldn't quite remember what to do next. Lucien came around to the passenger door and opened it. He extended his hand.

"Out you get."

Ben grabbed the lifeline and let Lucien pull him from his seat and into a hug.

"You really are out of it, aren't you?"

"Mmm." Lucien was warm. Ben wanted to stay in his arms forever.

"Let's go, Ben. The sooner we get home, the sooner I can get you into a hot bath."

That sounded good.

"Can I have bubbles?"

"If you start walking, yes you can. I'll even light a candle if it makes you happy."

The walk took longer than usual. Ben held Lucien's hand and dawdled along, humming.

"You're a cheap date if it only takes one glass of bubbly to get you this buzzed."

When they finally got back, Lucien left Ben sitting on the bottom of the stairs while he ran a bath. Ben sniffed the air and caught the scent of lime. He followed the delicious aroma and arrived in the bathroom to find it full of fragrant steam. Lucien leaned over the tub, swishing the water with his hand.

"You have a cute arse." Ben giggled.

"And you are a happy drunk. I should never have let you have alcohol on an empty stomach."

Ben stood unresisting while Lucien undressed him, peeling off the rowing kit and tossing it in the general direction of the hamper.

"I'm getting in the bath with you, or you're likely to drown." He stripped, and all Ben wanted to do was run his hands over all the sleek muscles.

"Come on, Mr. Grabby-Hands." Lucien climbed into the bath and sank beneath the water. Ben clambered in and sat with his back pressed to Lucien's chest.

"This is heaven. Thanks, Lucien." Ben felt a small pang of doubt. He should have thought of Lucien and what he needed.

"Whatever you're thinking, stop it," Lucien said. "You just got all tense. Relax. Let me look after you."

That was an easy order to obey. As the effects of the champagne gradually wore off, Ben enjoyed the long soak. His sore muscles unknotted as Lucien soaped him down and shampooed his hair. Lucien made no advances, just treated him with tenderness and care. It was one of the most erotic experiences of Ben's life.

Ben added 'making out wrapped in a towel with his lover' to his list of favorite things to do. Lucien treated him to a thorough kissing, then sank to his knees on the bathmat and brought Ben off with a mind-expanding blow job. Ben offered to return the favor but was firmly rejected.

"Later, love. That was for you."

Once they were dry, they dressed in comfy sweats, stopping to kiss between each item of clothing. They headed downstairs, then bumped hips in the kitchen making sandwiches. To Ben it seemed that the missing pieces of his life's puzzle were finally slotting in to place. They ate at the kitchen table with the radio as accompaniment. Conversation seemed unnecessary. Ben cast shy glances at Lucien and every time found Lucien staring right back at him.

Once they were done and the dishes piled in the sink, Lucien grabbed a bottle of wine and a couple of glasses.

"Let's get comfy in the lounge. I'll light the fire."

Ben curled his legs into the corner of the sofa and finally felt he could relax. The weight of responsibility that the race had put on his shoulders was gone. It was just starting to get dark, the fire was soon blazing and he couldn't imagine being any more content. Lucien handed him a glass of red wine and clinked his own glass gently against it.

"To us."

"Us." Ben lowered his eyes, suddenly shy.

"You were amazing today, Ben." Lucien tilted Ben's chin up and kissed him tenderly.

"I wasn't the one bleeding all over the boat. How did you manage to row through the pain?"

Just for a moment Lucien seemed distant, then his eyes sparkled and he was back. "Let's just say I was taught to control my response to pain by a very motivational teacher. I'm looking forward to giving you the same lessons…if you'll let me?"

He sat down and pulled Ben's head onto his shoulder.

"Yours, remember?" Ben whispered softly.

"As if I would ever forget." Lucien stroked Ben's hair gently. "Are you afraid?"

"Of what?" Ben didn't tense up but his voice sounded just a little uncertain.

"Of a future with me."

"As long as you don't decide that what you need is a submissive little slave boy who'll call you Master and sink to his knees every time you appear?"

"Hmm." Lucien gave the appearance of thinking about that quite seriously until Ben elbowed him. He chuckled. "Well, I can't deny I quite like the idea of that. You'd be naked, of course, and collared — something in nice, stiff leather…"

"Fuck off!" Ben twisted around and examined Lucien's face for any sign that he was serious.

"Maybe just when we play, then? I haven't forgotten what you said yesterday."

"That was in the heat of the moment, Lucien."

"So you didn't mean it? You said I could do anything…"

"I know I did…but…"

"But nothing." Lucien placed his glass on a side table and slid his hand under Ben's waistband to grasp his cock. "I have the evidence in my hand. Just thinking about it makes you hard."

"I… Oh God!" Ben bit down on his lip hard. "All right! I did mean it! Stop!"

"I didn't hear a safeword, Ben."

"Oh…" Ben moaned in bliss. He spread his legs.

"Wanton brat." Lucien squeezed Ben's balls. "No coming until I say so."

"Lucien, I can't take any more… Please let me come." Ben didn't care how pitiful he sounded.

"No." Lucien smiled wolfishly. "We have the rest of the evening and the whole night to get the rhythm right." He pressed a finger against the spot behind Ben's balls and rubbed. The sensation was maddening.

Ben bucked, arching his back.

"Besides, I think my stroke rate still needs quite a lot of work."

About the Author

Lucinda lives in a small village in the English countryside, surrounded by rolling hills, cows and sheep. She started writing to fill time between jobs and is now firmly and unashamedly addicted.

She loves the English weather, especially the rain, and adores a thunderstorm. She loves good food, warm company and a crackling fire. She's fascinated by the psychology of relationships, especially between men, and her stories contain some subtle (and some not so subtle) leanings towards BDSM.

L.M. loves to hear from readers. You can find her contact information, website details and author profile page at http://www.pride-publishing.com.

PUBLISHING